The Way of Wildfires
and hard luck believers

Brian David Cinadr

Wet Cement Press

Berkeley, Asheville, Reno

The Way of Wildfires
and hard luck believers ©2025
by Brian David Cinadr

ISBN 979-8-9918692-2-5

Library of Congress Control Number: 2025932621

Streetlights like Stars

Wet Cement Press
1908 Yolo Ave
Berkeley, CA 94707

Thanks . . .

This book is about luck, and luck it seems, the good luck and the bad, all add up to a life. I'm lucky to be surrounded by a mishmash of artists and writers, musicians, and photographers, athletes, masters of martial arts, doctors of thought and practitioners, jacks of all trades and just plain capable mother fuckers that can seemingly do anything they put their minds to. Every one of you is a bit of me and more than I deserve or could ever repay.

Steven Bergstrom, Kai Taylor, Pete Dack, Aaron Delgrolice, Orion Lee, Dr. Roy Page, and the TRUE family, thank you all for keeping the wheels rolling and the dogs fed.

Azi Shladovsky, Andy Summers, Rob Bragin, Liz Dubelman, Paul Slansky, Kimberly Brooks, Don Chadwick, Dana Stevens, Cathy Colman, Lori Altman, Brian Kaufman, Patti Connolly, Jordan Levin, Joe Levin, Chris Moore, Joshua Weinfeld, Rob Roberts, what could I see if it wasn't for your sight?

Barbera Roether, Thoreau Lovell and Wet Cement Press, thank you for listening to the voices in my head and making it all rhyme.

And Miwa and Sorcha, everything started with you, you walked me through the fire...

for Sorcha

you don't have to know the way to find your way...

It was the end of the continent and the beginning of
dreaming, the start of a California and of a salt water,
what was the first water and the beginning of blood.
It was the end of me, the first time I fell inside her, I
thought I'd fall forever, her legs and arms like long grass
and even the city was quiet, her apartment on Bundy,
her telling me she loved me standing in the door. But
love is like that, though it's hard to say what love is, like
a sun shining on a moon and on my arm out the driver's
side window, in her hair as if it wouldn't shine anywhere
else, as if it would only be day, the day we drove the 1 to
San Simeon, just married, a blue blue ocean behind her
like a lifetime, a lifetime like the old door jams in the
house, painted over and over until they were white.

It was a time of believing, but faith is for the faithful,
I'd lived on muscle, on ligament and bone, by luck. Yet
this place could only happen by chance, Los Angeles
was a village of smoke from the start, a city that should
have never been more than a town, a sunshine lie when
we came for the weather. We've always gone west, but
it seems now there's no place left to go, with the rents

the way they are and the beach traffic. There is an air that it's all too late, what's pushed the waves down and the breeze back out to sea. There are thirteen wildfires burning in the three western states, seven in California and four in Los Angeles County. The weather is calling for more winds today and for the next four days, but who's to say what's next.

They say Christ will come when it's time, I suppose there's a time for everything, what the Bible says, what the little man says to himself, scratching the date in his arm. He is awash in the t.v.'s flicker, in the dicker of his little daydreams, in the toy memory of his mother's pleasant thoughts, "Think pleasant thoughts," she'd tell him before she tucked in his blanket and turned off his bedroom light. He is here, where he has always been, where men like him always seem to stand, in front of us so we never see them, in the white noon sun on top of them so they don't even make a shadow. He is nowhere and everywhere at once, a man of medium complexion and build, five feet six to six feet tall, twenty-five to for-ty-five, driving some sort of pickup truck, black or even blue. We watch his dreams on the constant cable news and shake our heads and shout "why?" We imagine we don't understand him and hold him up to our own little secret hopes and fears and anonymous Facebook likes. A small man can be as big as God these days, big enough to be on the t.v. or even the Internet. It is the time of man. It is his time, when the winds start, what brings him to life like the dust kicks up.

We have colored the sky with smoke, a four billion year old sun muddled over with just two hundred years of man and carbon, what the little man has let out of the trees and the burnt brush in just days, the horizon stained, not even black, but a medicine of yellow, what we'd only swallow if we were sick, what will surely kill us before the cough. There are ten thousand things before this and after. We can only think of one thing at a time. It seems we are all of us always in the middle, never thinking it's the beginning or the end. It is the human condition that we suffer from hope, that we blame the hap on bad luck and the good as God's will. Everywhere there are ashes, it hasn't rained for months, not since the day after the Rose Parade. We should've known it was all too easy, blue skied day after day, somewhere down in our bones we did. The weather is the soul of a place and souls should never come easy.

**YOUR FUTURE IS
SUNNY AND BRIGHT**

PEKING NOODLE CO

The day I turned nine months I stood up and walked. It's a story my mother told again and again like it was all she ever knew about me, what my father only remembers as something that was hers and not even his or mine. It seems I've been walking since. I went west with no real reason, but reasons are hard to come by these days. We all do, I think, stand up and make our clumsy ways, our paths wrote out in DNA, in wrung out spinal fluid and elbow grease. Roads go two ways, streets always stop, men walk and talk of the weather, birds fly and sing, fish swim without thinking.

I'm sitting where I always sit, in the same Chinese restaurant in a line of Chinese restaurants, what crowd and crowd into a Chinatown. I'm trying to breathe, suddenly conscious of each breath. A long, pale fish in the tank next to my table swims to stay alive, living to live, pushing what water it can thru its sides, thru its cold blood, past its dark eye that saw it all coming. It moves with a grace that defies any desperation for it, swimming in a big glass tank that's too small, all of it from end to end, with only room to turn round and back again, always where it's just been, hopeless and religious. I fumble with my chopsticks.

I think of her for no particular reason, her hair and the cashmere sweater she wore, my brief reflection on the tank glass, the long fish swimming in a circle, what seems like a line, its body waving like a kite on a string, but I suppose we're all tied to something. I watch it swim alone despite the other fish in the tank, back and forth like the beat of a life, turn and turn like an earth or a moon, someone I knew once, and wonder where I've been and if I've been here before. The long fish is a dragon fish, a Chinese fish and good luck. It is ivory like time gets, I guess, and older, before there was land, maybe, back to when there was only water. It's been here longer than anyone remembers, the squint waiters and the broad mouthed hostess, the Lucky's original owner, a father I'm told, has long since passed and passed on the business to a son, now a daughter. No one knows the long fish's years, but some questions cannot be answered, only asked, as if to prove there's a God. The beginnings of things are always hard to come by and the ends we don't want to think about. But time is no matter here, the long fish is going nowhere, calmly and patiently, a Buddha on its path, knowing this, like everything, cannot last.

The glass tank that keeps the long fish is built into the wall so you can see thru to the other side of the restaurant. There's two sides to the restaurant and a kitchen in the back that's secret except for two metal swinging doors that give it away. It comes to you in an instant, like any tragedy or first love, an incantation of shouts and bouts of tough talk, clangs and bang clatters, private matters behind a manner of Mandarin and cutting knives, pot handles and pans, a man with a large tray just coming out the out door, another waiter and an arm full of dirty plates going in. The rooms are carpeted, but I've never noticed. The walls are painted a color you cannot see. The windows face Hill Street and the sidewalk like all the eyes in this Chinatown, the cheap clothes and the bags of fish, crinkled fists around American cigarettes, it seems the men all smoke and bet and roll dice. The women stut and stutter like sewing machines, stepping smally, only shyly, always looking down and looking up, watching their saucer feet and where the men's cigarette smoke goes.

I'm told the literal translation is "the house that brings good fortune," of the sign that says "The Lucky House" in black letters under six red Chinese characters, but everyone calls it "The Lucky." I don't know what the Chinese call it between themselves and their wound top talk, but I know what they order and order the same. The old Chinese men have a long ago knowing of nature and know the nature of things, their tight eyes wandering over the tanks 'til they put a crooked finger to a bound lobster today or a picky crab, mussels and oysters, shrimp fried in the shell, always the black bean sauce, everything served with the heads on staring back at you so you know just what you've done, some bit of fate or old men in brown polyester pants and flat shoes, bifocaled glasses in metal frames, choosing life and death like that...like $11.95 Gods that can only take.

14

It's hard to know why some things die and some things live, how things are found and lost again. There seems to be no sense to any of it, which explains it somehow, what the same waiter at "the Lucky" always says, smiling as he pulls a crab out of the tank. I worry now about all the things I've killed, ants and all the spiders, a bird once when I was twelve, a lucky shot, what the dull neighbor boy said as he dimly took his bb gun back and shuffled home. It was a small brown bird and no particular color, a mother, I suppose, and brittle like birds are. I wonder where it went, where they go and get to, all these bugs and birds and last loves, these women we never seem to know. I wonder sometimes if they're waiting for me, all of them crowded into some kind of heaven or hell or maybe just the corner of my eye. I sometimes think if I turn too quick I might see them, something out on the edge of my sight, out where the black of night and reason say I can't see anymore and everything I see for sure blurs and turns to a gut feeling and I go on believing it was nothing.

I wish I could have it all back, all the wasted moments, all the scraps of time I stuffed in my pockets like loose change I could have spent, all that time when I could have been in love. Patience is the good lie we tell ourselves waiting, mistaking pining for love. Love is Godly, heartache a common cold, a residue of what was, ticket stubs and valet receipts, her old number wrote out in blue ink on a fortune cookie fortune, back when she lived on Bundy, an avenue or a street. If I could somehow start again, be young again and full of chance, then maybe, but second chances are never quite so clement as our eyes closed and luck is a matter of moments of time. It seems every breath we take is by chance, this life a slim shot at the truth. They say art is truth, and art is dead, painters and poets, rock stars and Los Angeles...

I don't kill anything now, the killing done for me, cleaned up and neatly packaged and named so you'd never know anything was killed at all, free-range chicken, farm-raised fish, grass-fed beef. And still I catch the spiders in a cup and put them outside like some sort of offering, to whom or what I don't know. The flies I leave to fly around, all of them always battering themselves at the windows until I find their bodies on the sill the next day. It's strange how they live almost electric and how the life just goes out of them. There's crickets in the house, it seems they're under the refrigerator and in the walls. They're supposed to be good luck, what Lucy at 'the Lucky' says, but luck is a funny thing.

> **THERE WILL ALWAYS BE
> LUCK IN YOUR LIFE**
> PEKING NOODLE CO

"Thanks for seeing me, Hannelore."

"You're welcome."

"I didn't think you'd take me back."

"I'm here to help people, Michael, I'm not here to pass judgment on them."

"I'm... really sorry."

"Apology accepted. So, what's been happening in your life? It's been... let's see... almost seven months now since I saw you and Kelli."

"Kelli and I split up."

I promised her and probably no one else, it's what made us feel precious, like something she'd only take down from the high shelf in the cupboard for the holidays. But the canyons are burning and the black that remains has become somehow more important than the part that burned away, what we'll sift thru for the rest of our lives and after. I don't know what to say that this affliction of time hasn't already said. I can only pray her pith never wanes or falters, that the angry silence between us can last longer than the quiet indifference that is sure to come. I don't deserve any better, we both know that now, what I probably always knew, but I loved her first and promises can be like that, what she was convinced of and I couldn't quite believe. No one I think even knows me now and somehow without her, I can't know myself. It seems all I know is how to beat the stoplights on the Coast Highway and where to get the best Mexican or Chinese.

"I...don't know what to do."

"What do you want to do?"

"I want to make Kelli love me again."

"And what makes you think Kelli doesn't love you?"

"She moved out, she left not long after the last time we saw you."

"What do you think you can do to change that?"

"I can't keep doing the same old shit I've been doing...I know that. I don't know how to live...without her."

I'll say the words 'without her,' but I won't hear them, a part of me still believes in us, I'm Irish, on my mother's side, and the Irish believe in ghosts. I hear things in the house, echoes of where the furniture was, the ache of the wood stairs, a creak of elbows and knees, the bone rattle of my sleep at the window screens. My head is filled with memories and a tangle of dreams I dream each night, what I forget by morning and live with like some quiet disease that's killing me. And all I can do is think of her like all this water I have to breathe into, what I have to do to stay alive, all this blood I have to keep or die, a knot I can't loosen less my sap run down the road and into the creek somewhere, down the canyon to the ocean with its legs spread.

I may never see her again, I can see her in the oak chair in the kitchen crying like she would, and a time after when she wouldn't cry again. The rest of her sitting on the side of the bed with her jaw turned tight and her feet perfectly to the floor like she'd never lie down again, like she could never be anything else, but sitting straight up or anywhere else, but then.

"Don't assume Kelli doesn't love you because she's moved out."

"I don't know what to think anymore."

"There was…a lot of hurt between the two of you."

"If I can't make it work with Kelli I'll never make it work with anyone, you know. She was more than I could dream up."

"Have you talked to Kelli about coming back into therapy with you?"

"No. I know she kept seeing you for a while after I…stopped. I was hoping maybe you and I could kind of pick things up from there?"

"Michael, I'm obligated to maintain a client's privacy whether Kelli is active in therapy or not."

"It's just that you're…you're my only connection to her now. She isn't going to come back, I know that. I was hoping that you and I could work on things…"

Years turn to salt and snot and a poison that ruins our joints. I've lived a lifetime of years, four years with Kelli and fifty-three now when I add it all up. All of it pushing out of me like ten gallons of water in a two gallon bucket. But it's never the time, not really, but the miles and miles, the memories, the clothes she wore still in the closet, Polaroids and color photos stuffed in a drawer, birthday cards and candles in the cupboard, chipped dishes and wishes and what she said in the end, what we made with our eyes closed, everything like it wouldn't stop or happen again.

"I'm happy to work with you, Michael, but you have to want to do this for yourself."

Our house was an old house, something built before the road, something hand-set on bedrock, on dirt and mountain rock, what was under an ocean once, what is here now like it was never anywhere else. Nothing was plumb or square, everything was painted over, nothing worked, not even the fireplace. I suppose Kelli saw me the same, a charming fixer upper with a view, but she wound up breaking me if I wasn't already beyond repair and in return I broke her so she'd look like me. I think she loved me by the way I made her cry. I know I loved her by all the blood.

"Have you told Kelli you're coming here?"
"No."
"Are you and Kelli talking?"
"No."
"Is that your decision or Kelli's?"
"I tried talking to her, but…every time I'd call she'd just cry and say that it was too hard and I finally gave up."
"The truth is, Michael, you and Kelli had so much baggage from your pasts that it's not really anyone's fault."

"I hurt her…I know that."
"Do you love her?"

I can only nod yes as if I say it I'll break in two, holding the weight of it all up over my head like some cracked circus strongman at the end of the fair. I have nothing left. I am an empty hand. My three swings to ring the bell used up, my pockets turned out.

"I can't live with all the mistakes I've made."
"We all make mistakes….we're fragile creatures, Michael, even you, under all that muscle and that tough street persona."
"If I could have another chance, you know."
"It's hard work, most people never take it on…"
"I owe her that much."
"You owe yourself."

I promised her, a flower garden and a walk-in closet, but you always keep more than you have space for and the flowers go to seed. It seems the breaking is a part of any promise, like any life and death, the one draws the line around the other. It's what I think now, I'm not sure what I thought then. It seems everything is broken now, but even before these days, what we'll look back on and call the end, the porch boards were growing crooked and dry rotting to where we didn't dare walk anywhere, but straight in and straight out the door. I thought maybe all this would save us, but love does that, crossed fingers and picked up pennies. I've read all her books, the books she left like some bit of good luck, and the book

I always promised her I would read. I don't know if it's too late, but they are old books and their time gives me hope.

> **BETTER TO TAKE A CHANCE**
> **THAN HAVE NO CHANCE**
> PEKING NOODLE CO.

This is the beginning. This place is the end of things, of Marilyn and Morrison, the edge of west and all this America, an ocean always and always. This is what we've been waiting for, what has been ceaselessly waiting, what I feel in my blood when there's nothing else, water to water, salt and salt, the pull of the moon and Pisces. I hear it at night, the waves at my windows, what you hear clear into the canyons after all the traffic and the cell phone signals in the air have stopped, something that is somehow everywhere and nowhere else.

We come here to be from somewhere, to be someone amongst the millions and the streetlights like stars. All of us on Sunset or Sepulveda, Hollywood Boulevard or the freeways, Mulholland and the Coast Highway like a story we've been told again and again until it's ours to tell. All of us in the same sleep and a late September, a California dreaming and a coming heat. Everywhere the weather and the long afternoons of shadows, the hills in the distance thru the smog and the sun off the cement, the cement runoff running to the ocean like a secret everybody knows and never even whispers.

"Mister Michael, you not want all these things?"

"Go ahead, Elena, take whatever you want."

"You have these things long time, no?"

"Yeah, I guess, but...I don't know, it seems like it's time for it to go."

"What about misses Kellee? All her nice things she leave?"

"It's okay Elena, mine and Kelli's stuff, all the boxes, just take 'em, take what you want and give the rest of it away. There's some decent stuff in there."

"I so sorry, I thought this time it be good, misses Kellee the best of them."

"Yeah she was...I guess you've seen them all."

"First mama and then Maria, now me, twenty years we clean for you."

"How is everyone?"

"They good."

"I'm glad, tell your mom and your sister I said hello."

"I will, we pray for you, pray you be okay."

I can't remember how I got here, the Midwest highways all looked the same, flat shouldered and wide hipped regardless of where you are. I remember Texas though, and parts of New Mexico, what wasn't there more than what was, the space between things and the miles, the hum of the car's tires and the county roads, dirt roads that ran up to the paved road and went on into a paperback of horizons, lonesome telephone poles and blackbirds on wires, picked fields turned to mud. There was a way then, two ways if you were counting, an upper and a lower route, the lower being what you took in winter if you were smart. And there were numbers we'd never seen before, the 44 and the Texas 20, and exit's with town names and no towns to be seen, only a filling station, maybe, with truck diesel and gasoline and road signs that said "next gas 82 miles" and "stop" and "yield" and signs that didn't say anything at all, curves and crosses and silhouettes of deer, billboards for the first Baptist Church and the Mitch Hall Chevrolet in Lamesa, signs that said something if you were willing to hear, if you were looking for forgiveness or a Silverado.

I remember the nights bigger than the long days, the road stretched out like a vast black lake we were swimming in, the moon reflected on the hood of the car, on the asphalt, the California state line in the headlights. There was a girl then, but every young man needs a push, a pull really, the gravity of something bigger. There was a girl, her smile across the top of a screw top bottle of wine, her toasting the the state line and the mile markers, the Joshua trees like ghosts in the lights of the trucks driving east the other way. Everything we saw was new, even the sky and the night and the milk spill of stars. Neither of us had ever been anywhere, but Ohio, Pennsylvania once when I was a kid, a car trip funeral for someone, a great aunt or uncle I didn't know and still somehow they were a part of me like a root from the neighbor's tree slowly pushing up our driveway.

We were cut down to the bone, the two of us, out on the edge of holy and felonious, her and me stuck with our every thought and the simple violence of our upbringings, talk of God and the voices in her head, in my head. We drove on into the desert, her old four door

Ford burning oil and dinosaur blood, me hanging my arm out the window to feel if the California air felt any different and wondering if anything would ever be the same.

We had made our plan in the heat of a moment, the last hot day of a Cleveland August night. It was too hot to sleep. It was too hot to do anything, but sit on the roof out her bedroom window and think while she smoked her long cigarettes and stubbed them out on the top of a used up Coke can. The nights had grown close in, closer than before, the dark all around us like it was something we owned. Everything seemed right up to our skin, some bit of the lake and the smokestack smoke in the air, in our lungs and in our blood by now. Her old man was in prison somewhere south of Cleveland, in Lima or Columbus, outside of Cincinnati maybe. I only asked her why once, but she didn't say. She had those kind of eyes that said almost everything so you thought you knew her. I was young and didn't know anything at all.

We were talking like you do in the dark, what can never really be said, confessions of what we did, lick lipped pacts and cumming promises, prayers spit out like spells, blood from her period. The only light was the lit streetlamp shining around her head in the window behind her, but angels never know they're angels and halos never help you see. She said she recognized me the first time she saw me, when she saw me come in the door of The Horse. She said it all felt like a dream, that she had this dream once when she was just a kid, when she was five or six and barely in her shoes. She said she dreamt she was swimming, floating really, happy in an ocean, not the lake, but some sort of saltwater and warm and Cadillac blue. She'd never seen an ocean or anything past interstate 71, but she knew it was something like a Pacific. She was by herself in her dream and in her sleep, and yet someone was somehow with her, somehow all around her like the sky, but you know how dreams are.... And dreamers. She said she'd been thinking about that dream the last few days, that it just came into her head again like things will. She said that it was probably a sign, that we ought to head out west, that her old man was getting out in spring.

She said she had a friend in L.A., some chick who could get us work, who had friends and a place where we could stay. It seemed we didn't have any reasons why or why not or anything but time, but you can't know what you have when you're twenty or twenty-five, there's so little time behind you. I wonder if we ever know what we have when we have it, how we somehow lose more than we find. It takes time to say no and time to know if you were right. No is never genius. Yes is the start of something. Yes is the femur of youth, and I was young and chance, we were, and too young to say anything else.

I looked at her and then back at what was left of the moon and said I'd go, with the moon waning like it was there didn't seem any reason to stay. She breathed out a breath she'd held onto her whole little life and whispered something secret in my ear, her white arms around my neck, her black hair in her face and in my face and forever somewhere in my story. She pulled me into the house and onto the mattress on the floor, tearing herself in half for me like there was no other way, and would again until I thought there'd be nothing left. It's what she did, what a woman does, what a man wants instead of love, what love does until everything is gone.

She wasn't beautiful or even pretty, but a dark wish we've all made, something even God must have uttered to himself. She was on the verge of breaking if she wasn't broken, so you loved her when you saw her, helpless to do anything, but fall. You'd find a way to find her innocent, we all did, and within the reach still of a folded dollar bill or a five, we did that too. Private dances were thirty then and two and a half minutes, the girls could touch you, but you couldn't touch the girls, house rules. But girls like that you won't ever really touch. You're it, no tag backs.

She did the day shift weekdays for the suit's at their long lunches with their clumsy business accounts trying to be cool, sitting with their crooked hard-ons packed in their bad suit pants, their dumb smiles that looked like the grills on the fronts of the Fords they drove, LTDs when they made it and dreams of the boss's Continental. She did nights come Thursday and Friday and Saturday and tipped out the house and me and brought her money home in an old potato chip bag that she poured out on the floor and counted, eating Peanut M&Ms and smoking Marlboro Lights until it all added up to something.

She was different than the other girls, something you could put your hand to, but wouldn't out of a kind of working man's reverence, like she was cut out of marble five hundred years ago, like she was made by someone's hands that were better than you, and painted paint white and whiter maybe, maybe almost blue. She seemed some kind of royalty, even in the bar smoke and the smell of sex and beer spilled on the carpet, the nervous sweat of the business men with their ties undone and the union salt in collared shirts, no t-shirts or uniforms allowed, a two drink minimum and a ten dollar cover unless you were a regular and an all right guy by me.

I was working the door for Dickie George who owned the Crazyhorse Saloon, what everyone called "The Horse," the biggest and best topless bar in the city according to the highway billboards to and from the airport. Dickie did a good living by the Benedetti family's blessing. Their relationship was old and simple, Dickie paying out a weekly tribute in a manila envelope to the family for their continued prayers and benevolence. It was the same bit all the clubs had to play and pay for, the Benedetti's protection and the goodwill of Euclid Beverage and Vending, the faith of the neighborhood, a burned down business occasionally and we believed.

Dickie was a bare wire on an old lamp you'd be afraid to leave on, wiry and wired, running round like a clock that didn't keep time. He wore fag shoes, he wore cowboy boots before, he drove a 280Z, snorted coke with his glasses off, said he couldn't see with them on. I was never sure who I worked for really, Dickie or the Benedetti's, but I worked the door with a menace I wore as sure as my arms out my sleeves, and a black leather trench coat over that come winter, L.U.C.K. tattooed across my knuckles on my right hand and a Celt cross on my forearm, a black jack behind the bar when the luck ran up. I had no hands for handshakes, but a nod hey, maybe, and always a look you over, up and down, and steel-toed boots if I needed to say anything more. I didn't fuck around. I pocketed a part of the door, it was to be expected, Dickie didn't pay shit, five bucks an hour, fuck you. He called me in the office after my first few weeks and asked me if I was taking money from the door. I told him 'yeah' and that he was lucky I was handing him what I did, twelve hundred for a Wednesday. He asked me how much I took and I told him it was none of his business. He called me a son of a bitch and went back to cashing out the bar. We got along like that.

No one knew we were leaving, she and I, it was better that way, kept secrets are the kindest kind of cuts. I heard it said that it's better to be feared than loved, what old man Benedetti would say, what some thinking man said. I say it's best to be unexpected, everything ends, but fate. I'd make off with the door and the girls' cut to the club while Dickie was counting out the bar for the night, my last night in Cleveland, a last supper at the IHOP at the turnpike and Route 21. I counted out thirty-six hundred for us and a grand for the Bendetti's, if you knew what's right, an envelope on the eldest son's car seat, fear has its place. We'd make the Indiana line when no one was watching, while everything we knew was gray and sleeping, her and me dreaming our dreams out loud, awake, all our cash stuffed in my pants and her in her best dress, her only dress, a hippie sun dress and a long winter coat so you weren't sure if she was wearing anything underneath.

We crossed into California three nights later, the car clock said 2:14, but it was broken, had been for years, she said. I still think of it as when I got here, but time's tricky like that, made up and science. The long strung out road turned to a street and to the color blue, an end Route 66 and a statue of Saint Monica, a bluff and a beach. She kicked off her shoes and went across the sand into the ocean up to her knees, holding her dress up above that, the water too cold to go any deeper. I sat in the car and watched her like I loved her, like a wave, like anything that couldn't last, but rises and falls and disappears into the next.

It would rain just when I thought it would never rain again. The big lie of Los Angeles filling up the gutters and running in the windowsills, water under the door and leaking from the ceiling onto the bed. Nothing here makes much sense in the rain, like the sunshine makes it all matter. We'd go on like we did, for a while, but California was as far as we could go and some things need to keep moving to live.

I don't remember the year, but it was a Wednesday and a warm night so you wished it was Friday. We were eating take out Chinese, Moo Shoo Pork and Kung Pao Chicken. We argued over something, sort of everything, but her heart wasn't in it. We broke like that, softly and sort of all at once, but it was coming, quiet like a broken promise, things like us don't last. She moved on to some movie guy's pad in Malibu, six cardboard boxes in the back of her Ford and another four in the trunk. She wound up back in Akron I heard, to her mother's boyfriend's house, something like a bird, something to the sun and back to the summer gray of a great lake like it never really flew away.

It seems I never said her name then, her given name, a Bible name, something her mother took without asking. I say her name now like someplace I lived once, we all come from somewhere and are a part of some woman. She danced by Candy, sometimes, or Carrie or Sunny, something to keep us all guessing. You probably wish you'd known her, I wish I had sometimes still. It's hard to know where you're at until you're somewhere else. No one, it seems, is from here, not even the wind, what comes from offshore or in from Santa Ana. I couldn't say the last time it rained, it seems it won't rain now until November, if we're lucky.

DON'T WASTE YOUR TIME IN THE PAST, LOOK AHEAD

PEKING NOODLE CO.

"Hey, what's up, Tony?"

"Santa Anna."

"Yeah, it's really been blowing."

"Spirits very noisy last night."

"There was a lot going on, that's for sure. I didn't think the trees would be standing when I got up."

"There fire on 101."

"There were ashes on my truck this morning…it used to completely freak out Kelli, I think I've actually gotten used to it."

"Burn to ocean in 1994."

"I was livin' in Venice then, we got up on the roof and watched it burn all night…the flames went all the way to the beach."

"Burn since yesterday."

"You can smell it all over town, it must be pretty big."

"Very bad, wind not stop to day."

"I guess they've already lost some houses in Calabassas."

"I see on t.v. very bad."

"Hey Tony, is Lucy here?"

"Lucy in back, you want sit down?"

"Sure, will you tell her I'm here."

"Lucy very busy, stove not work right."

"Maybe I can see her after I eat. I need to talk to her."

"You sit where always sit, okay?"

"Yeah, thanks Tony."

"Okay."

No one comes to 'The Lucky' alone, there's only two tables for two. The other tables are rectangular tables and round tables, tables that seat six, even eight, ten Chinese, but they know how to hold their knees in, and in the middle, a lazy Susan, platters of squid and shrimp and a whole fried fish going around like gossip. If you watch and don't listen you can understand what they're saying, saying the same things we all say, what has always been said. I sit looking at the tables and the pat of the people and the food and the sounds of only Los Angeles out the plate glass windows to the street, to the sidewalk shuffled with faces like an odd deck of cards, faces I make up in my sleep that I only recognize now, the same man, always in the same white t-shirt, thinly carrying a box of bok choy into the Golden Dragon across the street, and the pinched woman who always watches him, and me watching them both. It's only chance that I see them again, but then I come here all the time.

"I told Lucy you here, she say she come out when she can, okay?"

"Thanks Tony."

"Okay, you want look at menu?"

"Na, I don't need it, what's good today?"

"Every thing very good."

"How's the shrimp looking today?"

"Very good, very fresh."

"Tony, you're so full of shit, you've been telling me the same thing for thirty years."

"It true, just bring shrimp in morning, still alive."

"All right, I'll have the shell fried shrimp in the black bean sauce."

"Alway black bean sauce, why you not try garlic sauce, very good."

"I like the black bean sauce."

"You full of shit, Michael, tell me same thing for thirty year."

I laugh like a man that has forgotten, that has been forgot. Laughing like these moments are all that's left of me and all that mattered in the end, a matter of minutes in a Chinese restaurant. Tony won't laugh, but smiles through his gold framed glasses, an honest smile full of gaps and metal crowns, a smile of cramped streets, of crowded alleyways without the sun, narrow places where back doors open onto shadows, where women shout down from fire escapes and thin men whisper to themselves and gut chickens. He walks to the kitchen with a satisfaction only poor men know, ten to an apartment, twelve in the apartment next door. Tony knows there's only room in his pockets for what he needs, wants are for rich men and wanting makes a man poor. Tony has exact change, rides the bus, sits with the people, all the hand me down housekeepers and hunched nannies, blue-shirted gardeners and day workers done for the day, Dodger hats at the highway off-ramp selling five pound bags of oranges to the traffic. All the people we won't ever see, only seeing what they do and what the sun has done to them. Tony can see, sometimes over his glasses without even looking, only a look on his face. Tony reads the Chinese paper, watches American t.v., says he wins at the Wheel of Fortune every morning at ten.

"Michael, everything good?"

"Hey Lucy, what's goin' on?"

"Burner not work, everything okay now, shrimp fried in shell right out. I have to watch repair man. Father tell me to alway trust people and alway watch anyway."

"It's probably good advice."

"You listen, Lucy know."

"If you have time, I've got something I wanted to ask you, you know, if you have time later to talk."

"Repairman check rest of stove and fryers while he here, when he done I come talk with you."

"Thanks, Lucy. I don't know what I'd do without you."

"No use worry what could be, only worry what is."

"…or what's not."

"Michael, how long you come here now?"

"God, Luce, I don't know, I started coming here when I was working security for Axel, that was like '88 or something, I've lost track."

"Time no matter Michael, every thing change and every thing stay same. I here everyday, right?"

"Yeah, I can't think of a time when you weren't."

"I here, but in different way, I change, too."

Lucy is a woman now and never a girl, but a boy before, a man once and strangely pretty, enough so to leave you uneasy, a small woman, what must have been a very small man. I'm not sure I'd know if I didn't know, not even her hands give her away, but for the eyes, maybe. A man's eyes are a lie and always so, so you know just what the truth is, a woman's eyes are a deep well, something we only see ourselves in and never the bottom.

Lucy was once Chen Lee, from a long family of men that could see, seers since just after the apple and Adam first opened his eyes. It was a sight passed on every other generation, Lucy's eyes like her grandfather's eyes, what were Lee's eyes once, eyeliner and mascara now, a thick blue shadow above everything else. It's said the men could tell a man's fortune by one good look in their eyes, knowing the exact second of a man's death, but only a man's, for a woman is a secret, even to God I think. Men make things with their hands, with dirt and water and fire. Women make men and the world it seems from between their legs, with a kind of magic, with blood and ghosts, things felt and unseen.

The Chen family stretched back to the state of Cheng and the first man, a shaman, named Chen Chi Hsien. It's told Chi Hsien had gone to gather water one morning where a beautiful fish swam just beneath the surface of an otherwise quiet pond. Chi Hsien looked into the water, into the fish's future and its long past, watching until it swam into the shadows, to where Chi Hsien could only see himself. He returned home with his buckets full, two buckets that by legend could never be emptied no matter how they were poured. The next day Chi Hsien went off to the mountain never to be seen again, it's said he saw his death and followed it. What we all do I suppose, knowing or unknowing, all of us aimed at our ends all along.

"Ni shi xiao tou!"

There is a suddenness of air, of voices, a vibration that can only be a fight from behind the kitchen doors that swing closed, a row above the usual raucous, a wire of a man, a white man in a gray button work shirt hurriedly coming out the 'in' door, an open toolbox red in his arms like an un-diapered baby. A startled waiter wanes from the man's path, bending like a blade of grass, he is studied and knows how to move with the wind and without it. The tray in his arms, however, is of the material world and burdened still with attachment and a stack of dishes from a cleared table, a folly of plates and bowls about to break, the sound before they hit like a wave curling under itself, everyone of us wincing before it all happens, the crash in our heads first, the sound only an echo of our expectation, the shatter like the air too has broke. Lucy comes out the 'out' door screaming in Chinese so you know just what she means, waving a fryer basket so you know she means it. Tony has a hold of her other arm, whispering something, ten thousand words in her ear, calmly counting off the versus of reason he knows well enough to have forgotten.

The repair man scrambles out the front doors like a bug might, like some species before history that only knows how to live, something you can't kill, but only pridelessly chase away. He trips down the sidewalk looking over his shoulder rather than ahead, the patch on his shirt says John, he thinks of himself as Jack, everyone calls him Johnny. His truck's in the back, in the alley behind "the Lucky," next to a Los Angeles city sign on the brick wall of the building that says 'No Parking Anytime.' Lucy and Tony walk back into the kitchen thru the 'in' door, though the doors aren't marked, it's known by those that know and followed.

There is a silence after, there is always a quiet under everything. They say there's a fault line that runs right under the city, what we're all waiting for to break like a frail old woman's bone. There are whispers, but barely, stopping when they're found out, everyone looking at everyone else as if someone's face might have the answer to what happened. All of us looking to Lucy when she comes out the 'out' door and then looking away as if we don't want to know, but it's sometimes easier to just believe.

"Jesus Lucy, what the hell happened in there?"

"Repairman, no trust them, alway try to take advantage because I'm woman, think Lucy not know how run business."

"What did he do?"

"When I come out to talk with you, he stick chewing gum in pilot light, tell me he have to service fryer. Tony see him."

"What an asshole."

"Yes, asshole...he have cancer."

"What?"

"Tell him he have colon cancer, tell him every time he steal money it get worse."

"Does he really have colon cancer?"

"Lucy never say anything not true."

"Are you ever wrong?"

"Don't know, story not over yet."

"But so far you're always right?"

"Alway."

"Luce, can I ask you something?"

"You just did?"

"You been hangin' around Tony for too long."

"Just joke, what you want ask?"

"Well, I sort of need some advice…about Kelli…you know, like…why do you think we didn't work out?"

"Everyone want know why, why too big question, people don't know what happen. First thing first."

"I know what happened, believe me, I can't stop, everyday and night it's all I think about, what she said, what I said…I can't forget it. I wish I could, it's driving me crazy. I go over it and over it."

"So what happen?"

"I don't think I ever understood her, I never knew what was going on inside her, she would just sit there and not say a word and that freaked me out, and when I got freaked out I lost my temper and that freaked her out and she finally couldn't take it anymore and left. It's what always happens, Luce. It's the same thing that's happened with all of them, Tracy, Dana…. I'm impossible to live with. There it is, you wanted to know what happened, that's what happened."

"Everything you say is why, you not know why. Say what happen?"

"Kelli moved out."

"Okay, Kellee move out, maybe Kellee not leave, maybe take step back, take look at thing."

"I'm not going to fool myself, she left because she didn't love me anymore."

"That because you try think why and you not see what happen, can't see why, Michael, only see what. So what happen?"

"She moved out."

"She move out. What it mean? Not know, could mean many thing, only Kellee know and maybe she not know."

"If you love someone you don't just walk away, you work it out."

"Kellee take all her thing?"

"No."

"She leave thing she care about at house?"

"Yeah, most of her things are at the house, she just took some clothes and stuff."

"You think she not care about these thing anymore."

"No, Christ she left all her pictures and her grandma's old vanity, but…I see where you're going with this, but she was in a small apartment in Santa Monica, it was just temporary, she didn't have room for everything."

"Maybe she love you, but no have room live with you right now, just temporary like you say."

"I don't know…"

"You know, you see what happen, don't try think why, need know what happen first."

"Luce…do you think Kelli loved me?"

"Can't see into woman, only see what she do and she do thing of person that love. She not talk to you because she have too much emotion, not because she no have emotion."

"Luce?"

"What else?"

"You know how I'm going to die, right?"

"Yes."

"Will you tell me?"

"No."

"I need to know, Lucy, I need to know when."

"Never tell anyone, Michael.... That not good thing to know."

"You told the repair guy he had cancer."

"He have cancer, that true, that not how he die."

"Oh."

"People know, but not want know, not really, not even Lucy, that why good for Lucy to be woman, look in mirror, just see face, and not know. Fortune need be surprise, that way you live you life. If you know you death you dying instead of living. You think you know thing, Michael, you not care if die, but you not know, there still many surprise. Need live, live you life."

**YOU WILL LIVE A LONG
AND COMFORTABLE LIFE**

PEKING NOODLE CO.

Life just happens by living, I guess, like luck, it's just something we own without really knowing how, something breathed into our blood before the big push. They say we breathe water before we're born, before the world and the rash of air. I wonder how we forget, how we struggle to swim again and drown in a dry world. Dying is the end of it, I know that, of this life. I don't know where it goes after that or what it all comes to, the hum that is somehow the oil of this living. Death seems to be the sum of it, like all these pennies I've thrown in a jar by the door. And someday, when I finally count them all, all I'll ever know is what they added up to, I'll never remember from where they all came.

I'm alone now, there are times when all of us are alone. People all around us counting the bones in their hands, counting their steps up the stairs to their old-paint apartments, reading the box of a microwave dinner in the dark and sleeping with the t.v. on. It's sometimes lonelier in the city, Los Angeles spread out to the edges of the orange groves like it does, car part stores and strip malls now, nail salons and Vietnamese takeout, everything where there were trees once, what is asphalt and concrete now, the memories of a thousand Chumash Indians under a Jack in the Box on Ventura.

"Big Mike!"

"Hey Butler…"

"Long time, bro."

"Yeah, you doing okay?"

"Livin' the dream, bro."

"Good to hear, man."

"You livin' at the beach now?"

"Nah, this is the closest market from the house in To-panga. What the hell are you doing over here?"

"Shit…I'm training some old lady in the Palisades, she won't come to the gym so we're working out at her house. I guess she was a big movie star or something back when they talked all weird."

"What do ya mean?"

"You know, old black and white movie talk, like wise guy shit, it's friggin weird."

"Yeah…I guess."

"So Topanga, bro, what the fuck, you gone all hippy on us?"

"Come on, man. Those days are long gone, it's all Au-di's and Range Rovers now. There's a few old timers, but it's the same Westside bullshit as everywhere else."

"You still got the SS?"

"Nah…I sold it."

"Ah damn, bro…shit, I loved that car, that ride was badass."

"Yeah, I kind of wish I hadn't let her go. The dickhead who bought it way overpaid me, but…ah fuck it, I still got the Chevy short bed."

"That truck is badass too."

"You still in the hood?"

"Hell yeah, bro, I ain't never leaving. Two blocks to the Strand and two to Gold's, as long as Gold's is there, I'm there."

"I heard some talk that Google's buying Gold's building."

"Don't even say it, bro, it's the mecca, it's a fucking landmark, fuck Google, they ain't shit…Arnold will buy it before he let's that happen."

"I don't know, man, things change, Arnold and Venice ain't what they were…."

Everything now is a perfect postcard sky, a prop of sunshine and palm trees, Prozac on the Westside, coke in the hills, the nil of the flat streets and legalized weed, meth in the Valley until all the stop lights turn green. I remember it all faded and frayed at the ends, the city stucco washed out and all of Los Angeles louder and smelling of sun on some girl's shoulder, Coppertone then, everything sun screen SPF 40 or zinc oxide now. They've cleaned up Venice, the Strand for the tourist, Abbot-Kinney painted mission white and colors and riddled with artisan, vegan, corridor shops, but the alleys still smell like piss. The drug deals that were dealt out behind the buildings, chronic and crack rock, whatever you want—they got—are somewhere else now, pushed inland and back down to Inglewood and somehow Electric Avenue is a thru street.

Hollywood has become what you thought it was before you moved here, dime shiny like a Disneyland and ruined with progress, only the Hollywood sign is in need of repair. Everything else has worn thin and been replaced, the music tin or maybe I'm finally too old, the Strip dim and lit with rich kids in dirty clothes ripping samples of every heartache their parents lit. Everywhere is clear skinned runaways blowing in the wind, ten thousand stories like litter on the sidewalks, but they're all fed and full and hopeless when they seemed on the verge of something once, back when they were hungry and had acne and saw stars.

"What the fuck, Mike, you quit workin' out or what, we haven't seen you at Gold's for like forever, bro."

"I just do some shit at home."

"What the fuck? That supermodel wife of yours not let you out of the house or what?"

"It ain't like that, man. I got canned from Epic awhile back, so I hardly come into town anymore."

"Fuck them, Mike. You don't need that corporate shit anyway. You want me to talk to Charles? He's been training Dre and all those mother fuckers for like forever, maybe they got something for you, you know? It's worth a try."

"No...I'm good, man...but thanks."

"Come on back to the gym, bro. The morning gang's all there still, Gilbert and little Mike, Joey, Stoney, Jerry, Steve...fuck, they'd love to see you."

"I miss seeing everyone, tell those fuckers I said hey..."

"Come on, Mike, what the fuck, you ain't workin'..."

"My body's not what it was man, you know, I got a lot

of miles on me, I can't do all the heavy shit anymore."

"Bullshit, you were a fuckin' bull, bro, it's still in there, muscle memory."

"Yeah, muscle memory..."

It was the belly of the eighties when it all began, everything metal band black, everywhere goth girls and new wavers, guns and roses rock and rollers, none of it would go far. Everything ended where it started, the whole world on the Strip and far enough to crash and burn and to be remembered if only for the hair and the make-up, the torn spandex and tattoos. Los Angeles was it, the Strip and the hills hip, San Francisco just old hippie shit, New York tired and turning. London punk had died on arrival, all the buildings burning down without them. The Clash split like school chums, The Police just quit, the gun at their heads, but they'd never pull the trigger. Sting went on singing some faint song of his own, but it was flab where it was tendon and bone before. It was 1986, almost '87, it was maybe just a day, a night really, something that couldn't last like the long legged girl in the back room, black eye liner and ripped black stockings. It was a bass riff that became our heartbeat and the heat of the lights and the black lit bodies that the air conditioning couldn't keep up with. Everything thru the smoke and the p.a. pounding like all of it and us were parts of one thing, part of the same animal, living and killing, giving birth and dying in a single night. It was rock and roll, it was the price we had to pay, giving up the days for night and a kind of life for another.

I always found work, I was lucky like that, twisting arms collecting cash or cars, working doors in titty clubs and rocker bars. I was working out in Gold's in Venice, the center of the muscle universe, Arnold and Franco and every mister somewhere Joe Blow. Terminator and Rambo were the biggest movies in the world. Muscle was it, everybody wanted arms and a box office hit. I was working the Roxy rocking like the Sylmar quake never stopped when it happened, the line of head bangers stretching down the street and around the corner beneath the billboards, vague models and the conscience of the Marlboro Man above us like twelve Roman Gods. I was baggy fatigues, all that would fit, and work boots, a white tight t-shirt and a faded raiders cap pulled down so you could only guess at my eyes, so you'd only know my jaw and the scar under my chin. I was walking six foot, two-twenty and lean like anything of purpose, the glean of a foundry town still around me, some bit of the molten iron and steel, some part of the coal smoke and what spilled into the lake, what made the river burn until it burned out and turned my blood to rock salt. The bands came out of the hills, out of the Valley and in the double side door, old station wagons and vans double parked on sunset, Vince and the Crue, Ratt and L.A. Guns, G n' R taking it as far as the bar and backstage 'til they were fucked up enough to play something.

I moved inside when things got heavy, to the VIP room upstairs, to the bent backed execs and their dressed up strippers, the black leathered rock star guitars and singers, actors acting cool, acting like they had cocks, smoking cigarettes with their hands like faggots instead of just lipping them like a man that needs his hands for work. If you went upstairs, you went up past me, a sort of Saint Peter at the gate, but I was no saint and upstairs was only heaven 'til two thirty and a sort of hell after that, hotel comedowns and the curtains drawn, brown bag men at the window, motel boots kicking in the door.

Los Angeles, it seems is where dreams come true, where we hope it never rains again even though we all know we need it. I was headed somewhere. I was a long way from where I started, everyone out here dreaming like they do, sleeping past noon, thinking the stars were two stories high, all of them never knowing if they were flying or falling. I guess luck just found me, I wasn't looking. I was just standing where I stood, on top of my feet like the old man taught me. I was in the scene, but I wasn't part of it, like a planet shining in some night sky, a moonlight or a moon shadow at the bottom of the trees, what is somehow here and only far away for sure. My world was between worlds, between the lights and the dark, the acts and the adoration, the press of the crowd and the stage. God is not among us, but above us, rock n' roll a religion of the religious. We can only love what we can't have. I kept the line between that love and knowing, and for the few girls made angels and taken back stage, heaven was a hard place.

TIME AND INNOCENCE ONCE
LOST CANNOT BE REGAINED

PEKING NOODLE CO.

This place is no place, not even nowhere or a corner, but a busy stretch between a freeway off-ramp and a street going west, like everything goes west, like east is something we don't want to think about, like death, like her with another guy. This place is someplace now, weekdays at one, an office in a building of offices, three floors of doctors and a dentist, a silent prattle of names in white letters on a black-backed directory board between the elevator doors. The walls are cinder block, where they're not drywall, and smoothed over with a glaze of paint and time. Everything like these buildings are, like they were, vinyl floor tiles in the halls and wall paper, metal windows that have oxidized, aluminum that's lost it's shine, a building that had promise once, something you heard, nothing you read, not in neighborhoods like these. All of it too close to the airport to ever be anything, but plastic backlit signs and broken asphalt, old cars for sale without the hub caps, single story ranchero houses with cracked tile roofs for rent.

There is a life behind the walls and in the ceiling lights, running wires and water pipes, a sort of sound, something that you somehow know is no good for you, something electrical, or chemical, sixties wallpaper paste and silicone caulk, sheet rock and fiber insulation. The only other sound the whir of blood veins, a rattle above the ceiling and behind the closed doors, something sole-ly human, a sound of walking up the stairs and down the hall. I sit waiting in the small waiting room alone, sitting in a chair, one chair from the door, something from a dead relative's dining room set, maybe, surely not office furniture, what smells of a grandparents' parlor, a coffee table and two odd lamps, two paintings trite with hobby, real art is life and death. The receptionist's window is dark behind its blurred glass, Hannelore has the office to herself now. Eight small holes in the door, the veneer faded around the place where two placards were, two names, and Hannelore's name still, what was the third name.

I always sit in the same place, I never think to sit any-where else, I don't remember where I sat when I waited with Kelli. The same woman walks out of the office ev-ery Wednesday, into the waiting room, into the hall, a gray lady always in a sweater though it's ninety outside, a hundred in the sun off the pavement. She won't speak, but to say goodbye, her back to Hannelore as she says it. She never looks at me and yet somehow, still, she looks away, both of us wondering what's wrong with the oth-er, what we've lost, if it shows.

"Come in, Michael. How are you?"
"Surviving, I guess."

The room smells of carpet, the smell of oil gone on to nylon or polyester, the smell of childhood visits to the doctor or the dentist, the worry of an elevator, memories of vaccinations and the threat of a cavity. It is the smell of commercial cleaners and candle wax, maybe Nivea, something that seems familiar. There is a couch and a love seat like an old woman might keep, like something she'd think she's too close to dying to replace. Hannelore is in her late fifties, maybe sixty, but younger by the blue in her eyes. She sits like she knows, straight up, 'til she leans in and says something, like everything she says are your words and no one else's.

"Well, everything changes, this time will change too."
"Do you really think things can change?"
"I do…that's why you're here, right?"
"Yeah, I suppose."
"Let's talk about when you met Kelli."
"It was different with her, you know, I'd never met anyone like her…but it wound up being all the same shit as the others. I guess that's because it was the same old me."
"You both had an idea as to how things would play out and you made that happen."
"So you're telling me I did this on purpose?"
"Not consciously, no."
"I loved her…I think she loved me…that has to count for something?"
"So why did things turn out like they did?"
"Why's a tough gig."
"It can be."

"I'm scared I'm…I don't know…trapped with myself."

"And what are you trapped with?"

"That I've got too much past to change…that it's too late."

"You can't change your past, but you can accept it. You can change yourself if you can see yourself."

I'm down, I've been down before, bouncing at dollar topless bars, downtown, downstairs, front doors and back doors, a thousand trespasses and those that would trespass against us, some big handed mother fucker from Akron who almost took me out once. There is a moment in any street fight when you can only do without knowing, some part of you that will only survive by being. There is a time before the first swing when anyone can win, a lucky punch is all it takes. And there are the moments after when you're down and you know the kick's coming, all of you gathered into a black around your spine, around the oldest part of you, something we all share, what runs thru us as men. And for that stab of time you are beyond chance, only a ghost and the ghost of all the men that made you, and you will get up and finish him or let go and be finished. I am down, I am beneath my skin and into my marrow bone, into my blood now, used up water run under the street. I am down, I am pure pain, but pure all the same. I don't know what this pain is for, but to make things clear. What you can't see until you squint and grit your teeth and rise up.

"Michael, let's talk about your childhood."

"I can barely remember it to be honest with you. My mom died when I was eight, I guess that was sort of a thing."

"What was she like?"

"I don't really remember...not remembering her, you know? Like she was always just something in my head."

"Well, what do you remember about her?"

"She had the whitest skin of anyone I'd ever seen... and black hair which kind of made her look even whiter...and glasses, like John Lennon glasses, you know, those round ones. Um...I don't know...um...she didn't really cook, she was always burning everything and we'd wind up scraping the black off and eating it or throwing it all out and eating t.v. dinners or something."

"What was your home life like when she was alive?"

"She came down with Rheumatic Fever right after she had me, so I don't think she hardly saw me when I was first born except for my dad holding me up at the door. I don't remember that, it's just what the old man told me. I do remember her being sick all the time, she was always in and out of the hospital. He'd come home and make dinner and leave for visiting hours while the neighbor girl watched me...Jesus...Stacy Matuzak. I haven't thought of her in years...."

"She was your neighbor?"

"Yeah."

"What do you remember about her?"

"She was pretty cool, she was really pretty, probably my first sort of crush...she ODd her freshman year at Kent State."

"How old were you when that happened?"

"I think I was in fifth or sixth grade..."

"How did you find out she died?"

"Her mom was crying in the driveway when I came

home from school. Our driveways were right next to each other. Mr. Matuzak told me that they'd 'lost their Stacy,' I still remember that, I remember thinking that it was weird that he didn't know where she was, I kept thinking, 'lost her'?..."

"It's interesting, our choice of words for death. So you're an only child?"

"Yeah, I guess they tried to have more kids, but my mom had a couple of miscarriages after me and then she got sick. That's what my old man told me. Really everything I know about her is from him."

None of it feels like mine, but a picture book story that was told to me line by line. A childhood of hand me down clothes, piped striped t-shirts from an older cousin and a pair of pants that would fit, something I could stand in, but still feel where their knees had been, where their bones shone thru. Mother is the picture the old man kept in his wallet, a Kodachromed moment between a yellowed plastic photo sleeve, a lock of black hair pressed into the shape of his hip, drapes a man would have never picked, tatty with time, barely hanging on as if he took them down she'd really be gone. The bath towels a faded blue, smelling of bleach when they smelled of fabric softener once, what makes me think of her, the only memory I own of her, really, what I keep secret so it's mine.

She was the old man's story and nothing more, a myth by the time I was ten and made up, but what do we know of our mothers anyway. They make us with blood and cum and a string of good luck, and grow us up and push us out, and we in turn make them, turning them into something other than a woman, something whispered in our ears from a heaven and not quite heard.

"How did your mother die?"

"A blood clot or a hemorrhage or something, it was some sort of blood thing on account of cancer…I don't really know, I was little, I just knew she was dead."

"And you were eight?"

"Yeah."

"And other family?"

"My grandparents all died before I was born. I had a couple of aunts and an uncle on my dad's side, some cousins and stuff, but they were only around on Christmas and stuff."

"What was your relationship with your father like?"

"He tried, you know, I mean he's a good guy, I just think after my mom died he sort of…I don't know, he never really got over it."

"He never remarried?"

"No."

"Did he ever have another relationship?"

"No, not that I know of, but…sometimes I think he might have had an affair with Mrs. Matuzak."

"What makes you think that?"

"Nothing really, it's just a feeling I got, I always go with my gut."

"Did the Matuzaks have other children besides…Stacy?"

"Yeah, Pete and Nick, but they were way older than me, Stacy was the baby…like by ten years or something."

"And Stacy? I imagine her death must have affected you?"

"She'd gone off to Kent and I was eleven or twelve...I didn't need anyone to watch me anymore once my mom died, the old man, he'd come home right after work. I suppose it was sort of weird, I don't know, I don't think I thought about it that much, you know the way a kid is, all you're thinking about is football practice or basketball or something."

"Tell me more about your father."

"I don't know what to tell you...he was all right I guess, he did what he could."

"What didn't he do?"

"What do you mean?"

"You said your father did what he could, that sounds a little...limited."

"He was always taking care of my mom when I was little...between her and him working he was barely around. After she died he was home, but...I don't know...he sort of...checked out."

My father stood standing and straight up, down hard on his heels, down into his shoes like he meant every step. But hard wood trees that stand straight will break in the wind, while soft woods bend and sway and save their sap for spring. Sometimes, I think, it's better to be weak than strong, sometimes. Sometimes it's better to give up and give in, to move aside and move on. A priest came to the house after my mother died, a heavy man with a red face and scuffed black shoes. He told my father that she was finally at peace, he told me she was living with

God now, like God had something we didn't, the old man and me in this shit house on Whitewood Drive. We never went to church again, after she died and the funeral. The old man had run out of prayers I suppose or believing the fifty cent candles were worth it, but like I said, hard woods break, oaks and fire maples.

"Did your relationship with your father change after your mother died?"

"Not really, I think he tried to be around more, but it's like there was no one left. He went to work and came home and made spaghetti or hamburgers or these fried baloney sandwiches he always ate and we'd watch t.v. and that was it. I don't know if he even watched, he just sort of sat there."

"Did you ever talk about your mother's death?"

"He'd tell me the stories I'm telling you...but he never talked about her dying. We didn't talk much really, I mean except for the Browns or the Indians or something...

"Were you home alone after school?"

"Yeah."

"Eight years old is pretty young for a child to be home by themselves."

"Times have changed I guess, it didn't seem like a big deal back then. I mean don't get me wrong, I got into my fair share of shit, but I could take care of myself."

"I don't doubt that, but a child isn't supposed to take care of themselves."

"It made me tough, you know. These suit's that I work with now, or use to work with, they're all a bunch of...well you know, they don't have any...umm..."

"Grit?"

"Yeah, grit…they wouldn't last a day outside of their Westside lives."

"Michael, your childhood undoubtedly formed in you a number of admirable qualities. From the little I know about you from Kelli and from our past sessions, you've frankly, come a long way, it's quite remarkable. I'm not sure you know that. But what you do know is that something's not working."

"I just want to be happy. I wanted Kelli to be happy…"

I heard a break, a rib I think, where I kept her, what I gave her, some part of my side, somewhere close to my heart, but hard. I wonder if she heard it, that last phone call, if it broke the skin, if she saw it, if Hannelore can see it, if breaks like this ever heal.

"You didn't really have a childhood, Michael, you were parenting yourself by the time you were eight."

"Yeah…I…I guess that's probably true."

"That's a lot of weight for a little boy to carry."

"It is what it is, I didn't know any different."

I can't look at her, I look out the insignificant office window instead, a burdened sky falls onto the back parking lot cars, onto the flat roofs of squat shops, and thin houses boxed in by side streets and garbage can alleyways. The mountains are burning. Somewhere a small minded dozer tacks a tree to the ground, a burning, one hundred and sixty-three year old oak, something magnificent and ordinary still, a humble saint pushed along a scorched ridge line until it's covered with ash and earth, until it's somehow not a tree anymore, but something else. And we will go on and never know what we lost and never find enough to be anything else but less.

"It's okay, Michael…. It's time to let that eight year old boy cry.

**A WORD OF ADVICE WILL
COME FROM A CHILD**

PEKING NOODLE CO.

Her and him, what became the two of them, were Catholic and still I was an only child, an instance of God's guile or an odd bit of luck, even after all those seeds, I seem to be the only seed that took. The rest, I guess, were blood clots and nothing more, what I was told, what they tell you when you're old enough to know something happened and too young to know what they think is the truth. The last one, the fourth one, tore the life right out of her, the stain still on the wood floor under the shag carpeting like a car trip souvenir we brought home and put away and didn't think about anymore, a Niagara Falls plate or a plastic tomahawk from the Serpent Indian Burial Mound State Park. Father Kovacek from Saint Basil's said they all had souls, the blood clots, and said prayers for them, and blessed the house and her and drove back to the rectory in an old rust colored car. It was strange to see him drive, like seeing God behind the wheel when you think he'd just fly home.

We lived on Whitewood Drive then and would, the old man lives there still somehow, like he never lived anywhere else. I imagine he'll die there, in their bed or the brown chair he sits in, waiting like the busted up mailbox out front, a dark thought I carry around like a rabbit's foot that he'll hang himself on the old clothes-line in the backyard someday. We lived with her picture on the wall like you might put up a picture of a Jesus. He lived on after and armless without her and legged along with something in him that wasn't his, a shadow on his X-ray, but that was years ago, a lung only half way now, where the darkness spread, but nothing seems to kill him no matter how he tries to hold his breath. He stayed alive all this time for me, I suppose, and now I stay alive for him. I call him once a week, every Sunday, five his time, two o'clock mine. We talk about the weather or the game or the standings in the American League Central and nothing that matters, as if nothing else mattered after she died. And he'll hang up like he always does and think how much I sound like her, how she was a fighter, and me, I'll think how he could take a punch and how he never took a swing.

I'm on the mountain or in the canyon, it's hard to tell which is which, what was pushed up out of the ocean and what was washed away by twenty million years of rain. I'm in the old house in Topanga, what was our house, what is somehow hers still, her flower garden and her grandmother's credenza, hung pictures and porcelain vases and the snug corner place she picked to sit in. It seems there's space now where everything was crowded before, in the closets she complained about and in between the floorboards, dust and DNA where her breaths were and the empty bookshelves like bones. I am what goes bang in the night, the rattle of the wind and the tree branches at the windows, a dog bark at the black. I am nothing anyone can see, not now, not without her, a ghost in the green house up the street or down the road, what the neighbors surely must think.

Kelli did what women do, lit candles and put the lights on at night, while all I could muster was to drink orange juice out of the carton with my shirt off and knock holes in the wall. The old man and me drank Coke or Pepsi or RC, whatever was cheapest, right out of the bottle, returnable bottles in a wood case we kept in the garage. He drank bourbon whiskey, what he kept hid in his closet, what he smuggled into the house from the Ohio State Liquor Store. He came home on Fridays from the plant with his clean uniforms for next week, "Mike" wrote out in red script across the left shirt pockets, "Ohio Crankshaft" in block print on the patch on the right, "Jim Beam" on the label on the bottle under his five shirts and five pairs of pants, everything on wire hangers inside a clear plastic bag. He was the only foreman that wore a uniform, that didn't wear a tie. He said he liked the guys to know where he started and that ties were dangerous around the equipment, but it was really so he didn't have to do the wash, but for his t-shirts, but for his underwear and socks, what he didn't have to fold, what he told me once shoving them all into his top dresser drawer.

My clothes are in a box in the closet now, most of the furniture is given away gone, the car, my Impala, a 497 factory V-8, Sixty Six SS, sold. A guy in the Valley dropped it and sprayed it its original mist blue and pinstriped it pearl and plied it with twenty coats of lacquer final.

"God damn, I loved that car."

I say it out loud, everything I say out loud I mean, even when I told her I loved her, I meant it, if not a promise, a sort of curse. All the suits at Epic drove "Porsches" or "SLs" or the new "7 Series Beemers." They never got it, but it takes a certain sort of man to understand the purity of heyday American horsepower, like Eden before the apple, double barrel carburetors were godly, computer chip fuel injection only after the sin and the fall of the big three in the seventies. I see it around town still, I sold it to some so and so post house hipster from Los Feliz. He paid twice the price I paid for it plus four times what I put in. He didn't even look under the hood before he handed me the cash. He said he had a sport coat the same color and drove away, the kind of weak backed guy that wears thrift store jackets and two hundred dollar jeans. I saw it parked in front of Dan Tana's just a few weeks ago. He'd hung a pair of fuzzy dice from the rear view mirror and changed the license plate to "MARTNESS." I had to fight the urge to rush in and pull him out of his corner booth by the lapels to the sidewalk out front and kick his ass.

"Motherfucker."

It's still my car, somewhere in time, if you buy into Einstein, but time comes and goes and certain times somehow never leave you. We all have our own bit of time, I suppose, a time and time to kill, what's still beating for you, what's dead and gone for someone else, for her, like her with some skinny European guy in tight pants, the two of them at your restaurant, what she thinks of as just a nice place by the water, his hand on her hand, her eyes on him like they were on you once. And you swallow hard and smile and live with the notion that he's fucking her, and he'll live with the knowing you fucked her first, we all do, us men. And you'll squint your eyes and bite down on your teeth so you don't flinch and tell them hello and how are you and look straight into her for maybe the first time and tell yourself you fucked her best.

I'm back to having almost nothing, most of my life I never had much, but life is up to chance and it's best to have nothing to lose if you're living on luck. It seems there's no mornings anymore or evenings even, but days and nights, blacks and whites, yes's and no's, streetlights along the PCH when there was only a moon once or the acid of a sun. It seems I've lost the things I tried to hold on to and what I let go has settled in place. I wonder if we really keep anything, but birthday cards and long letters I loved you, short notes hello and good bye, happy photographs that have curled at the corners and turned sad, a drawer full of what's gone on and gone bad. I've got my last month's severance pay coming and the cash from the Impala. The house is for sale for more than I could ever afford, what a lawyer said I'd have to pay out to Kelli. What I'll keep is in a few cardboard boxes in the bedroom and our bed, a couch we bought on La Brea, the stereo and the kitchen table and chairs. The rest is Kelli's, family furniture her Protestant parents picked up or gave away. It feels right in the end to have the house empty, like once you've puked you'll feel better.

I never bothered with the furnace with her not here, but I split wood for the fireplace and put on a second shirt, a flannel shirt or a thermal and sometimes a sweater over that. It seems colder here than Cleveland ever did, spaces under the doors and the windows where the wind gets in. Maybe it's me, maybe my blood's run thin from the years and the Santa Anas. They say the average adult male has five quarts of blood, maybe six, maybe I have too much, too much life like I got everything I was going to get all at once, no seconds. Maybe I'm bled out or maybe it all stops and I've somehow kept going. Cantor's Delicatessen is open all night, but the bar in the Kibutz Room stops serving at two. You have to wait 'til six am to start drinking again. But that was then, I don't touch the stuff now, not since I got the idea to get it done all at once.

DON'T PUT OFF TOMORROW WHAT YOU CAN DO TODAY

PEKING NOODLE CO.

"Thirty seven! Okay, you table ready."

Lucy never takes you to your table, she only nods over her shoulder like you know where you're going, like you'll somehow find your place, but everything does, what Lucy knows, all of us drops of rain in an ocean. We're born knowing, I think, our numbers and where we're headed to, heaven and hell wove into our still wet bones. Somewhere at our spines is some small part of the truth, some crumb of God that lives in us or all of us Gods ourselves, all of us doing what only a God could do or the simplest beast, a thousand lifetimes over and over until we remember to wash our hands and cover our mouths when we cough. I knew I loved her the moment I saw her. We knew it was over long before it ended, like the two of us were burning the furniture to keep the house warm. And still I'm surprised at the house being bare, at the spaces where she was once, an emptiness at the front door where she'd leave her shoes.

"Michael, how it going?"
"Hey Lucy."

"You meet with someone?"

"Nah Luce, it's just me."

Everyone is sometimes "I," sometimes "Us," sometimes "Them," everyone alone and unknowingly part of a crowd. It's hard to know what people think and what they think of you, what and who you are to a life that rushes by you. Me, I'm the sum of my hands, I suppose, fingers and toes, two thumbs that make twenty, what adds up to one. I've spent a life on my own, talking to myself, what the old man called my imaginary friend, what he told the neighbors, but I knew it was just me. Me reading cereal boxes out loud with my mouth full and the t.v. on, announcing the game, playing catch against the garage door with a Superball, baseballs didn't bounce. Now I'm a man, a married man according to the county, but the bed's only slept in on one side. I tell myself stories still in my head, in the car and in the house, since she left. Being alone is what I hate and what I do best, what the county doesn't know.

"Have table soon, you wait here, people there eat orange and go, already pay…other people big group, wait for round table."

There is a sort of line out the door, outside and down the sidewalk. A stacked deck of faces, all of them waiting, all of them in the middle somehow and me always at the ends, all of them in an order only an East can understand and stand in, a bow instead of just bending. Their talk is sudden and silent again, something not English, something about the wind and the smoke in the air. The men with their chins cupped in their hands, holding their arms with the certainty of concern, the women holding their hair and their purses.

"Very busy tonight."

"Lucy, you guys are always busy."

"More busy right now, Japanese tourist bus come."

"Yeah, I saw it out front."

"Too big, no place park on street."

"It's good for business, Luce, no one wants to eat in an empty restaurant."

"Too many Japanese, eat all the squid."

"That's the hard part of being you, you already know everything that's going to happen."

"Everybody know Japanese eat all the squid."

"People surprise you sometimes."

"No surprise for Lucy, everyone go where they alway going."

"You know where I'm going, Luce?"

"Yes, you know too."

"I don't even know what I'm going to eat?"

"Everybody know what you going to eat. "

"Yeah, well maybe I was thinking I'd have something different tonight."

"Szechwan prawn very good, pepper grow where my mother family from in China, long time recipe, but it no matter, you think all you want, then you have black bean sauce like alway do…Forty four! Okay, table ready."

We are what we do, what I've always thought, all of us doing the same things again and again and still I don't know what it is I've really done. I don't know how I've lived this long or how I lived thru these lives, theirs and mine and Los Angeles like it is, ashes everywhere now, what falls from the sky, what we have here instead of weather.

"Need keep door close!"

"I got it Luce, I don't think any of them speak English."

"Wind no good, Santa Ana bad thing, make people crazy."

"This town's full of crazy people with or without the wind."

"These strange day, more strange than usual."

"You feel something coming on, Luce? It is earthquake weather…maybe I'll sit under the table."

"You sit in chair, no earthquake tonight."

"Maybe it's the Japanese eating all the squid, you know, that's throwing everything off?"

"Not Japanese, too many fire, too much of anything mean something."

"It is weird, I can't remember a time when we've had so many fires."

"Los Angeles not balance."

"Well balance doesn't really come to mind when you think of L.A.. I mean, come on Luce, this place is completely whacked."

"Wracked in it own way, but now something not right…you house okay?"

"So far."

"How close fire to you?"

"I don't know, probably ten miles or something…the news said it jumped the 101 this afternoon, but it's all the way up in Malibu Canyon."

"What year Topanga burn?"

"It's been years, the big fire was '94, I guess."

"Nine and four together bad numbers."

"I suppose we're due."

"Tony say they bring fireman from other state."

"Yeah, they're flying them in from Colorado and Arizona, but it won't make any difference, it all depends on what the winds do."

"All thing up to nature."

"Do you think we have any say in any of this, Luce, or is it all just fate?"

"Hard to know what man and what heaven…twenty nine!"

It's hard to know what's burning in the hills, what will grow back as black as it is now and what's gone forever, sumac and scrub brush, needle grass and oak, its smoke miles from where its roots are, what we all leave in the ground, I guess. Eight people come in the door, what seems like fourteen, all of them with close wrought eyes, something different than mine and still the same, what Lucy knows as Japanese. The smell of the fire follows them in, a far off sin we're all somehow guilty of, what some fuck with a blue or black compact pickup truck started so he can watch it all on t.v., pissing sitting down with the bathroom door open so he doesn't miss a thing. The first man in, of the four men and four women, hands Lucy her number back, bowing and smiling, his broad face creasing and pulling apart. I watch Lucy write them down, their family trees in the backs of their eyes and in the back of her mind, what fills her thoughts whether she wants it to or not, their lives and deaths told again and again. I watch the long fish watch them, watch me and never seem to notice a thing. I wonder what it sees, seeing both sides with one look, praying back and forth, its eyes on each side of its head. The tank behind Lucy like a life once, a name then, something you said ten thousand times that you won't say again, but to yourself. Before Lucy is a simple wood stand with her numbers hand written and her spiral notebook, everything in Chinese, but the numbers…

"Lucy, I've been coming here for what, since Axel and the band, and I've never got what's up with the numbers."

"What you mean?"

"There's no order or anything, it's like they're just random numbers or something."

"Yes"

"Yes, they're random numbers?"

"Yes."

"So…how's that keep people straight?"

"Number random like people, but people number not random, everyone have number."

"People have a number?"

"Yes…when you first come here you have number, people you come with have number, number add up, write down in book and on ticket."

"Do I have a number now?"

"Yes."

"What is it?"

"No need to write now, you come here very many years, you know without number, you sit when it time…thirty five!"

The last six on Lucy's list step into the Lucky, the sidewalk empty, six lives in this one life, six numbers, what is thirty five by Lucy. The couple I was waiting on, rise and walk by, whispering some mad poem between them, the man with a white plastic bag, the red on the folded paper take-out containers showing thru its spell, pagodas I think, what I know really and never thought about. I move past them, past Lucy and the long fish, towards the table. Bobby is taking away the couple's dirty plates, what's left of a whole crab and a whole fried fish, broken shells and picked out bones, tea cups and a tea pot, chop sticks and two small bowls for rice, white, steamed, what they didn't leave, but for a few grains for luck.

"You too slow, mister Michael waiting...

"It's cool Tony, there's no rush."

"You miss place on table...there...there, you too sloppy for this job."

"You're doing fine, Bobby...Jesus, Tony, you're turning into a bigger ball buster than Lucy."

"Need watch when Lucy busy, he slow all night...lazy from easy American life."

"Bobby, is that true? you living the American dream?"

"Yes, very good sleep."

"Sleep?"

"Wo de meng ting hao de"

"What's he saying Tony?"

"He say he dream good, he like America very much."

"You both need work now! Tony! Bobby! Kai shi gong zuo...Michael you know what you want? I take you order."

"I thought you know what I want, Luce."

"Szechwan prawn and shrimp in shell with black bean sauce."

"How'd you know I was going to get both."

"Lucy know, she... Tony! Ru guo ni tou lan, ni shui zhao shi wo sha le ni. ..."

"What's she saying? Tony."

"She say..."

"Tony!"

"What'd you say? Luce."

"I tell him to finish his work or I kill him when he sleep."

"Oh."

"You not know... Tony been here too long, think he know, but he not know shit."

"That's pretty deep, Lucy, give me a second to sort of absorb all that..."

"You think Lucy funny, but it true, he know more long time a go, now he think instead of just be Chinese."

"You know, I've been thinking about what you told me the other day, you know, about trying to see what happened instead of why."

"You like Tony, think too much, you need just be."

"I've got to get my life figured out."

"You do every thing hard way."

"How's that?"

"You want know what happen with you marriage, you want know why thing go wrong, but you can't see mountain when you standing on it."

"What do you mean?"

"You try see what wife see, like you try see every part of mountain when you stand on it, that hard way."

"Okay…so what do I do?"

"Answer where question is. Wife question, go where wife is, talk to her now she away from you, when away you see all of mountain with one look."

"I guess, but it's…complicated."

"Not complicate, you want answer, then ask question."

"Then I'm back to why and you tell me why's are no good."

"Why not question for earth, why question for heaven, what you want to ask on earth that you not know answer to already?"

"I don't know…Luce…Jesus! I gotta think about this shit…"

"Thinking not alway good thing, sometime better to not think, wait and see. What you need to know come to you. Grandfather say try not know anything and you know everything."

I'm listening, looking straight at Lucy until I realize and look away, but not before her stare stabs through the whole book of my life, from the first page to the last, all my life just like that, my fate wrote out in embryonic fluid and cast in aluminum die. And in the smallest chance of time I can see all of time, the beginning and the end and finally grasp that it's the middle that matters.

I glance at the long fish, its left eye on me no different than Lucy's eyes, a brief shard of sunlight in a greasy alley and time enough still for us both to know what I've always known and asked anyway.

"Lucy…do you believe in bad luck?"

"It hard to know what bad and what good, Michael. Hard to see small thing and big thing…time change thing. Better to wait and then see…"

DON'T WORRY ABOUT SMALL THING, SEE BIG PICTURE

PEKING NOODLE CO

All of us here are always waiting, all of us in our cars, in our little lives and luck. We all want to know what's ahead of us, twisting up our necks like birds to see, an accident or some sort of road construction, LAPD maybe, searching thru some poor Mexican's busted up Toyota truck. It seems we're never quite still or really getting anywhere we haven't already been. All of us always starting and stopping, choosing between surface streets or six lanes of traffic, trying to decide whether to roll the windows down or to keep the windows up and the air conditioning on, wondering what burns less gas and what's the best way there, wondering what lives are lived out on the other side of the freeway wall, what Google Maps doesn't tell you.

Maybe this city is something you can never see, fog at the beach and smog in the Valley, all the people in this life only driving by and by, all the people always on some number, the 10 or the 110, the 101 or the 405. This place is ten thousand places, ten thousand names on the same t.v. news, six stations, and the same old story told six times. Everywhere here is like a dream you won't remember, what you'll only know was a restless sleep, Silver Lake and Los Feliz, Echo Park and Culver City, Rampart and South Central, West Los Angeles and East L.A.. Everywhere here is a myth except for this or that traffic app, except for the radio traffic report every twelve minutes and the mundane murders counted up in the Times.

"Hello! hello, yes, it's right over here…"

She dreamed then, before all this, before this kind of life you can only die in. A life like the stacks of newspapers she's saving to read or the old television shows she turns on and off now. She's not quite too old, but between, between retired acceptance and surrender, between relief and any real sorrow. You know her, we've all lived here once, all of us are between things sometime in our lives. All of us for a year or even nineteen months in some sort of off-white apartment, a rust stained sink where the faucet drips and the vague smell of gas from an old hunched over stove. You know her, the woman that watches thru the blinds, who listens thru the walls, who talks to the t.v. set thinking all this is a part of her life, what she is only a part of like the junk furniture you didn't bother to move, a plaid couch you left on the sidewalk, a fifty cent garage sale lamp and a coffee table you found next to the dumpster the day you moved in and brought back inside. You know her and nothing about her really, nothing, but her desperate wait for the mailman and the funny smell when she opens her door for the kid selling candy bars for the Santa Monica Boys and Girls Club.

"I'm sorry, I…"

"I'm so glad you're here, I've missed all my morning shows…the cable thing-a-ma-jig…it's on top of the television."

"Mam, umm…I'm not a repairman."

"Oh."

"Sorry."

"I was so hoping you were the Spectrum Cable man…I don't suppose you'd know anything about these cable television boxes?"

"Not really, sorry."

"Of course, I don't mean to bother you…but with all these wires and such…it's all too much for a woman my age. I guess I'll have to wait for the experts…I was just hoping I wouldn't miss my afternoon shows."

"Maybe everybody's is out, you know, if you weren't doing anything besides changing channels it's probably not you."

"Oh my, so you think this might be a whole city-wide dilemma? Oh that could take…why I don't even know…days, maybe even weeks to fix…I'll miss…oh I can't even think about it."

"I'm sure they'll have it fixed in a couple of hours."

"I'm so afraid the repairman came and went already, the numbers in this building are so confusing, I can't tell you how many people I see wandering around in the courtyard looking for this apartment or that…Bill won't have a number on his door, never would, he'd take it down as soon as Hector would put one up, he's the Mexican handyman that works for mister Solomon, Hector that is, not Bill, Bill drove the number nine route until he hurt his back, it must be…twelve, thirteen, fifteen years…oh it can't be, can it? Clarice passed on in '85, then there was that college girl, actually two of them, then Bill…I was never one for numbers and math and things…there's no three if you're looking for three!"

"I'm here at number 8, thanks."

This is where Kelli went, where my mind wandered to, where my thoughts fell like dust and the everyday around her, her standing at the bathroom sink washing her face in her hands or brushing her hair at the edge of the bed like she did. This is what shook out of my dreams, what all this sleep came to, an old address on Fifth Street, her maiden name on the mail slot written out in her handwriting with a blue pen. This is where we end, her and me, what was us. Me in my head, at an arm's length, in a thumbnail house, on a mountain in Topanga. Her in a courtyard apartment building, in a neighborhood of courtyard apartment buildings, in the flats before the bluffs in Santa Monica.

In beach towns like these the old buildings all have names, names like the Oceana and the Tropicalia, hers the Wonder Palms wrote out in wood letters on the side of the building so it seems to have mattered, what they did back then, just after the war. The rest of the building is stucco painted pink and sun burnt wood trim, what was painted green once, like a paperback book with the pages torn out, what only leaves you guessing at the end. Her apartment is on the first floor, a corner, the building two stories and storied with lives and a variety of luck. Breaths that moved in and out and others that could only end here at 500 Fifth Street, the widowed woman that fed the feral cats in the alley or the thin man that never married, who trimmed his mustache in the mirror with scissors and a comb, what he kept because the secretary at work told him in passing she thought it would look good once it grew in. What he had since 1971. What his sister had the mortician shave off in 1998.

"Are you a friend of Kelly's?

"I'm Kelli's husband."

"Oh I'm so happy for her!"

"What I meant was…"

"It seems just the other day she was going thru that awful divorce. Things move so fast these days."

"Well yeah…um I guess you're right. It does feel like it was just…yesterday."

"That explains why we haven't seen her, why it must be months now. I'm sure you went somewhere wonderful for your honeymoon. Were you married in Minnesota?"

"Michigan…Kelli's family's from Michigan."

"Of course, well I'm so glad she met a nice man she can be happy with, she went on and on about you and your yoga studio…and, well you know her first husband was in…the mafia."

"Kelli said that I…that he's in the mafia?"

"Oh don't worry, I've never seen him here, not even once. He lives way up in the mountains somewhere…Tahoe, I think."

"Topanga."

"Oh, well he never comes here, he's probably in hiding."

"I guess Kelly will be moving out. I saw an older woman taking her clothes out not long ago, the poor thing hardly has any furniture, not enough to bother taking I guess…"

"Most of her things are still in Topanga."

"…there's a lot of that here, people coming and going before you even know their names, leaving all kinds of things…Hector takes it all down to the Salvation Army store, some beautiful things too, kitchen tables, perfectly good couches, plant stands…you name it, though I suppose he keeps the good items for his family. Not that he doesn't deserve it, he's such a hard worker and he has the dearest family, very devout Catholic, all of them, I can't count them all, I'm just so horrible with numbers…"

"Yeah…I guess we're all living in a sort of…disposable society now."

"It's a shame, but at least it doesn't go to waste."

"Well, it was nice meeting you."

"Oh yes, I'm so happy Kelly found a good man, she seemed such a dear thing and so young to have gone thru all that…Is she back in Maryland still?"

"Michigan."

"Right, yes Michigan. It must be beautiful there. A woman from Iowa or Indiana, one of those states like that, I have the hardest time with geographical things, she moved into number nine for a short time. She just hated it here, all she could talk about was how Illinois was so much more this and so much more that than Los Angeles. She moved back after four months, mister Solomon let her out of her lease, he's a good man like that…. She left a gorgeous geranium and this redwood planter, Hector brought it over, he knows how I love plants."

"It's very nice."

"It's grown quite a bit since then, it must be…I don't know…four, five…seven years now that I've been taking care of it. I suppose I'd have to return it to her if she ever came back for it, I'd be just sick having to part with it now."

"Well, after seven years I think you can consider it yours."

"I'd hate to get in a legal battle over something so close to nature."

"I think you're safe."

"Do you think so?"

"Yep…well…I better get going…"

"Oh, yes, I must be keeping you with my prattle. Are we going to see Kelly again? Surely she must be coming back for a few things."

"I don't really know what's going to happen, things are sort of…up in the air right now. Like you were saying, everything happened pretty fast."

"Of course. Well, please tell her I said hello and congratulations."

"I will."

"I was so hoping I'd see my shows today, I've been following these terrible fires all week, it's just awful."

"Yeah, it's not looking too good."

"*Entertainment Tonight* said Mel Gibson's house might be threatened."

"Well if it burns to the beach we're all in trouble."

"I lit a candle for him at Saint Monica's this morning and for all those poor firemen, they're doing such an amazing job. You know they saved Cher's home the last big fire like this, she said the flames came right up to the driveway."

"Yeah, what they don't tell you is her driveway is a mile long."

"I was thinking, if it's not too much trouble, that maybe you could check and see if Kelly's television is working?"

"If it's still in the apartment I will, but I don't think there's much of anything in there."

"Of course and you're trying to tie up loose ends. I must be keeping you, I'll be fine, I'm sure the cable people will be here anytime now."

She steps back into her in between, back behind the ache of the screen door, her face and her flower patterned dress fading into a kind of gray, not even a black, the sort of shade that grows in courtyard apartments like these. She'll try the t.v. again, there'll be nothing but horizontal lines and static. She'll say a prayer just barely out loud and wait for a change.

I wonder who she thought I was, who he is...

"Fuck..."

I feel like I might puke on the steps or put my fist right thru the cheap door, the thought of Kelli with someone else turning my insides to black, the kind of thing that will kill you in time if you don't get it out or do yourself first. I can't think. I can't think about it now, any of it, when or how, what with the in between woman watching, I have to be cool, like I've been here before. I've been here before, if only the part of me Kelli took with her, what I gave her, what wound up being all I had. I've been inside her, four years and a year before that, what ties us together for this bit of forever, after that I don't know.

I bite down on my teeth like I used to, like I did when I was just a punk kid, when I was ready to fight, fix everything tight and harden up my jaw. I open the screen door and hold it with my shoulder against the spring pulling it closed. I reach up, there's a key above the door, flat down on the door frame like I knew there would be. There's likely another, with a neighbor or the manager, surely there's one with her friend Gia hanging from some ridiculous key chain, Kelli always concerned herself with things like spare keys. I hesitate or that's what I'll tell myself, how I'll remember it, but I've known I was going to do this all along, like Lucy said, we all go where we're going. I feel the key into the keyhole and push the wood door into the dark of the apartment. The air is burdened with time, with the smell of Pledge furniture wax and the weft of worn thin bedding. It is ordinary, I suppose, a compounding of days, the smell of every old apartment and something more still, what you can only remember and forget again, an ancient memory kept in a seemingly purposeless organ in your side, something instinctual, spiritual even, if you believe in such things. There is some part of us that is just ahead of us, what makes a person look over their shoulder when we come in the room, what we leave behind, the essence of our beings or a brand of shampoo. She is here, some part of her, some thread of us all unwinding.

"Kell...fuck...I miss you so much...I'm so...sorry."

I'm talking to myself, maybe to her, to anyone but God, that would be a prayer and I'm surely undeserving. There is a kind of silence hung on the walls, if I listen, where her pictures were, the nails left in the plasterboard, what is somehow more stark than if the walls were bare. There is a quiet between the hush of the cars on California and further away on Fifth, if I hold my breath, a space you can hear after each sound, the sound of someone walking across the floor above. Maybe it's the refrigerator or the timbre of the whole world at once, always a sort of hum when it's quiet so it's never really quiet. There's only the necessary pieces of furniture, what feels temporary, a cheap IKEA couch and a bookshelf with unlikely Viking names, two kitchen chairs and a flimsy kitchen table for four, a mattress and a box spring, a metal bed frame holding them off the floor. The apartment like an old rusted out body of a car stripped of its parts, a cup in the kitchen sink, a pile of junk mail and papers on the floor by the front door. Nothing here is a part of us, everything here is after me.

Maybe I'm no different than the old woman across the courtyard, maybe that's why she saw me when no one else seemed to notice, each of us living out some in between, what was green, what isn't brown yet. I sit down on the couch and breathe, holding in the apartment air, holding Kelli inside me, what's left of her if anything, atoms and ideas. I sit and think, I can almost dream, of where I am, of when we were still together, of when it was just Kelli and me, and now it seems we're not even at the end, but past.

"Fuck…"

I am nothing now, but a string of gut, of muscle tendon and a kind of what-for of luck, what you can't help but notice, a limp and a gait still that will get you, bone and sinew, a Notre Dame medallion and faded tattoos. It always seemed to me that this was when I was really ready to fight, once I'd lost, but you never really win a fight, you live and are a little less because of it. It's the fights I lost, I think, that I somehow walked away with a little more.

I get up off the couch, my ghost pressed in the cushion, a shadow from my feet across the floor, but I can't say where the light is from. I put a fist, a right cross, thru the drywall, lucky that it wasn't lath and plaster like these old buildings can be. It's what she'd expect of me and I'm not man enough to let her down. I won't feel the sting, only the ache later inside my hand. I close the door behind me, careful to put the key back like it was before. I notice my breathing, the air awkward, wondering if the water might not be easier. I walk around a banana tree and a fern and a palm growing in the center of the courtyard to the in between woman's apartment and knock on the door just below the two. It somehow makes everything okay, the magic of Catholic or karma, my silent sorry. Her voice from right behind the door.

"Just a minute…"

"Oh hello, are you done already?"

"Yeah...I thought I'd take a look at that cable box before I take off, maybe you won't have to miss those shows of yours."

"Oh that is so kind of you, I don't know where the cable people could be."

"Well you know the way these cable guys are, they're all a bunch of fu...well you know."

All of us here are always waiting, it is the nature of Los Angeles, what once was a village of Indian smoke, el pueblo de nuestra senora la reina de Los Angeles, a haze that hung between the mountains above a river that has since turned to cement. The water is all in bottles now, the smoke it seems is all that's left, what hangs over us all still.

WHAT NOT THERE SOMETIME
MEAN MORE THAN WHAT IS

PEKING NOODLE CO.

"Michael, come in. How are you?"

"I went to Kelli's."

"Okay…well, it sounds like we're going to have a lot to discuss…so did you and Kelli talk?"

"No."

"Did you talk before hand."

"No."

"So you didn't have any arrangement to meet?"

"No."

"Was Kelli home when you showed up?"

"No."

"Well…maybe that was for the best. I think it would be a good idea to give Kelli her space…and that goes both ways, I don't think Kelli should come up to the house in Topanga without some sort of okay from you."

"I don't think we have to worry about that."

"You never know, people can surprise you. That said, it must have been difficult to see where Kelli's living."

"She had her maiden name on the mailbox."

"I wouldn't make too much of it…"

"Nothing is even final yet, not legally, it's like I never existed or something."

"I don't think she did it to hurt you, it's not something she'd necessarily expect you to see. It is her place."

"Yeah, it's her place, I just pay for it."

"I assume that's something you and Kelli talked about before she took the apartment."

"We were supposed to be taking some time to get things figured out, I guess she got it figured out a little faster than me."

"What makes you think that?"

"I had a nice talk with her neighbor while I was there, she thought I was Kelli's boyfriend, 'the one she's heard so much about', a fucking yoga instructor...Jesus!"

"Who told you this?"

"This crazy woman in the apartment across the courtyard."

"Well, consider the source."

"She seemed to know a lot about Kelli."

"Even if it is true and Kelli is seeing someone, it doesn't mean she's happy."

"Fuck it! I don't even know why I'm here?"

"You're here making yourself better. What Kelli is doing is most likely the same thing she's always done."

"I think she tried."

"You made things untenable for Kelli, but she played a part in that too."

"I know I need to do something, but...I've got a right to be pissed."

"Yes, you have a right to your emotions, of course, but you need to recognize what you're really feeling. You came back to therapy because you know you need to change."

"And what if I can't?"

"You can do whatever you put your mind to, you've proved that."

"I don't know, Hannelore. I feel like…rage sort of fuels everything I do."

"Don't confuse passion for anger."

"But how do I stop feeling what I'm feeling?"

"I don't want you to stop feeling, I want you to reinterpret what you're feeling."

"Well, I'm feeling like I want to tear the fucking yoga guy that's fucking my wife in half, call it whatever you want."

"And what's that going to do for you?"

"I don't know, I don't know anything else."

I am back on my own again, back to my blood again, down to the bone, to what makes me turn in my sleep and whir like a hornets nest. Here I am where I've always been, in the same old circle and the family stone, back to yours and you, what I lived and lived thru, what I've never really forgot, beget, begot. But you keep what you run from, I suppose, and let go what you face and finish.

I'm in my head, in her hollowed out apartment, in the old house again and again, after school, waiting for the old man to come home, waiting to hear she's never coming back, her or her, memories that grind in my joints, in my gristled elbows and knees, a history of empty space in my periphery, what I can still see even when I'm looking straight ahead, so I can't see anything without it.

"Okay…so where does all that rage go? "

"I swallow it…well…now I swallow it…don't get me wrong, I cracked plenty of skulls in my day, but I always hated it. I know that probably sounds whacked, but it's like throwin' up. You know, you don't want to throw up, but you know you sort of have to and you stick your finger down your throat. Either way you're gonna feel like shit."

"And what about afterward, after you've swallowed this anger?"

"I don't know."

"Well to use your analogy, you can't really get it out by getting it out, you're poisoned either way."

"Yeah, it's pretty much always there."

"If someone punches you it hurts, right?"

"Probably, I mean some guys punch like flies, you know they got no ass behind them."

"It might not do damage to you, but you feel it, nonetheless, no?"

"Yeah, I guess."

"Is it safe to say that if someone punches you it makes you angry?"

"Yeah, I can put up with a lot of shit, but once you cross that line and lay a hand on me, I'm going to bust your ass in half."

"So when you hear that Kelli is seeing someone its like she took a swing at you…emotionally, Kelli packs a pretty big punch."

"Yeah, I suppose."

"The problem is whether you fight or not, you still have to swallow it. That doesn't seem fair to me."

"It's all I know."

"Would you say, from your past as a…professional bodyguard…"

"That's a nice way of putting it."

"However you want to refer to it…from what you've seen is a person who's in control likely to win a fight with someone who is out of control?"

"Absolutely, I used to just watch these guys get all crazy, taking wild swings at everything, they couldn't do shit…they'd always get their asses kicked."

"Exactly, you can't control your opponent, but you can control yourself."

"I'm startin' to wonder about you Hannelore, you seem to know an awful lot about fighting."

"I am a marriage and family councilor…oh! that's horrible."

"You know I always thought you looked familiar, you worked the door at the Viper Room didn't you?"

"Well you have kept a sense of humor through everything."

"Make 'em laugh, make em' breakfast…"

We all have our story, some cheat sheet version of the truth, what we keep in our pockets so we don't get caught, but deep down we know what we did, broken windows and door dings, swings and misses, back seat weekends and bottle promises, and all the white lies to try and get the stains out. Everything we've ever done and everything that's been done to us dusts the space between our bones, what makes our joints crack and our backs ache.

Hannelore laughs, then we both laugh, and for a moment we're free like school kids home on a snow day. But a poisoned sun is in the window and somewhere, I don't know when, my laughing turns to crying like there was hardly ever a difference.

"I'm sorry…"
"You don't have to apologize, Michael."
"I still love her…"
"I know."

I loved her like I did, like something I'd won, like something I could only lose. They say you can't take it with you, but where would I go after this, after Los Angeles like it is, one blue-eyed day after another. This place is the kind of beautiful you knew was no good, what you tell yourself different because you know you can never leave her, the kind of girl that can only leave you. Only she can wreck you and save you, love you and forget to call you, keep you with French kisses and kill you with a sharp turn in the weather. Wanting what you can't have is surely divine, trying to keep what you have, the devil, what raises us up and drags us down, angels and Los Angeles alike.

**YOU SOMETIME WIN
MORE BY LOSING**

PEKING NOODLE CO.

It's hard to know what you have and what you're stuck with, what you shook off and what you lost. There's ten thousand things and ten million people, all of them with a past and a future that's longer than all of their lives laid end to end. What we share and cannot touch, what we had to lose to get here. Los Angeles at the end of everything as if this is where we were going. I can't say where it is we're headed, there's 12.2 traffic related deaths a day, what the California Highway Patrol statistics say. I wonder if we're not all ghosts driving the same road, the same time everyday. Everyone rolling along on fossil bones, on animal oil and old tree sap, talking in the air on mobile phones like magic, like they'll never be alone again.

"Bobby…qu ba zhuo zi ca le li gan jing…"
"Dou bu gan zi ji de huo, dou yao wo lai gan."
"Ni men dou tai you xian le, wo dui ni men tai fang song le."
"Wo bang Tony li zhuo zi, ta tai man le."
"Hey Michael, how's it going?"

"Hey Lucy."

"You sit, have table ready, five minute."

"Thanks Luce, there's no rush, I've got nothing, but time these days."

"No time, time illusion."

"Okay, then I've got nothing."

"You finally learn."

"I don't feel like I know a damn thing."

"Have to know no thing first, then room to learn, you listen to Lucy, you be fine..."

Lucy knows now and the end, our ends and hers by heart, what curves her smile slightly downward at the corners and the set of her stare somewhere past us. It's an odd thing, I suppose, to have read the last page of the book first. I wonder if any of us would even bother with the rest of it if we always knew how it ends.

"Tony, ni tai man le, tai you xian..."

"Zhuo zi hen hao."

"Ni tai lao le, bu neng zuo zhe ge gong zuo le."

"What's going on with you two?"

"Tony tired, want to go home."

"He's probably been breaking his back all day...Tony, what time did you start today?"

"Not matter, all day an night not enough for Lucy."

"Michael, you not know, Tony lazy, he need go back to China, remember how to work. I send him myself... Hui jia shui jiao."

"Wo hai you gong zuo yao zuo."

"You zuo de geng hao de ren."

"Tony, how many years have you been at the Lucky?"

"Before Lucy…wo zuo wan jiu hui ja."

Tony turns and takes a large tray to a larger round table, to what's been left like a thirty dollar room, eight people's dirty dishes and a stained table cloth, eight dollar bills laid out like a slept in bed. He and Lucy will not speak again tonight, she'll take a man's pride, but knows to leave his hands and feet for work. Tony's shoes are worn thin, the bones along his back poking thru his white button shirt when he's bent over, his back curved with time and all his arms have held and hurried. He is a piece in this gravity, a branch that has grown dutifully long, what bows to the ground now instead of up at the sun. He clears the table thinking of each and every plate and bowl, glass and cup, fork for the white people and plastic chop stick, what click and clack together like old ankles down a stairs as he gathers them together into a handful. It is how he bears the weight of this everyday, the tedium of tap water, of air and the in and out of it all. He is here and nowhere else, the rest of us always trying to get somewhere else so we're never really any-where.

"So, Tony was here before you?"
"Tony work for father, that long time now."
"When was that?"
"Father die nineteen eighty eight, lucky number."
"Not so lucky for him, I guess."
"Maybe lucky, who know?"
"Yeah…so Tony's been here since the seventies?"
"Nineteen sixty nine."
"Jesus, Luce, that's a long time."

"Tony work hard then, too old now, need stay home, watch teevee."

"I can't imagine the Lucky without him."

"I put his picture on wall."

"Come on, Luce."

"He too old, but I let him stay, I too easy. Father not easy like me, everyone work hard when he here."

"Sorry, Luce, but 'easy' isn't exactly the word that comes to mind when I think of you."

"No, I too easy. Father alway say, you need be hard, hard work good, if you easy people not work hard, you not help them succeed."

"I think your father would be pretty happy, Luce, I mean, look at this place, it's packed every night, what else matters?"

"How thing done matter...I too easy, I fail them, they not know satisfaction of exhaustion."

"There's something to that, I suppose."

"It true, you work hard, thing okay. Look what happen now you not work, everything no good, you too much time to think."

"Well Epic had a little say in that."

"That not work, you need work with arm and leg, shoulder and back, everything else follow."

"I've done enough grunt work to last a lifetime."

"When you come here long time ago, you happy."

"Things were simpler then."

"You work hard then, maybe you need remember exhaustion too."

"Maybe. Maybe my life got too easy and now I'm paying the price for it."

"Easy no good. Air condition car, air condition office, people separate from nature, even Lucy in air condition restaurant."

"No one's going to be in here eating if it's a hundred and ten."

"Lucy too soft."

"Valet parking and bullshit twenty-two dollar Stilton blue cheese burgers and twelve dollar truffle oil fries. That's soft! The Lucky ain't soft."

"Hard to live right in this city."

"You sound like Bruce Springsteen."

"He monk?"

"Sort of…"

"Monk not know life now, now ask for money instead of food."

"Them and everyone else."

"You have no thing until you have no thing. When you have no thing, you find ten thousand thing."

Lucy was born in an east, in a sort of dream at the foot of a mountain, in a field so it looked as if she came right up out of the ground. She doesn't know the year, but she knows the season and that the moon was waning and not a time for planting. She doesn't know the time of day, but why look for what's not there. I wonder if she has a man or a woman, if she's ever been in love, in all these years I've never had the nerve to ask. She seems in a different world than me and still she is here, and me, I'm off somewhere else, at the bottom of some ocean I can't see or swim in, dragged along by an indifferent current.

"You know Luce, I don't have the fight in me anymore...not like I had..."

"Need give that away too, you be okay, stone still hard, sometime stone cover with moss."

"No Luce, I'm tired, you know?"

"You mind tired."

"My body's tired."

"Body follow mind, you think too much, you fight you own nature."

"Whatta ya mean?"

"You not know who you are, maybe now you learn."

"That's just it I don't...I don't know what I've learned. I think things are different, that I'm different, but it's always the same damn thing. I don't know what to do."

"You need find true self."

"Yeah, but what does that mean?"

"You need go work again, work with hands."

"You want me to go back to banging heads again? You're crazy."

"Good warrior fight when time to fight, come home and plant rice when war over."

"So you want me to...plant rice?"

"You want rice, go super market. You want know self, answer in you heart, only way to heart is with hand, need work with hand, work hard."

"Work hard at what?"

"You not know with head, but you body will know."

"Jesus Christ, Lucy, why do you have to make everything so damn difficult all the time? My head hurts by the time I get out of here."

"You learn by hard thing in life, not easy thing."

"Come on Lucy, help me out, I mean what good is it seeing the future if you're not going to use it."

"No help to tell people life, can't tell you life, need to live life."

"Just this once, Luce, come on, we've known each other almost, what? Thirty, thirty five..it's more years than I can count."

"Okay, Lucy tell you what you need do next."

"Finally...okay, cool, let me have it, I can handle it."

"Go sit down, you table ready."

"Awe shit. Lucy, come on!"

"More than you know when you come in."

"That's a pretty slim slice of future, what about after that?"

"Order Szechwan prawn."

"Can you give me something that I can use outside of this restaurant?"

"Need try different thing...no black bean sauce like alway...and eat slow, chew food forty time, good for you chi, you eat too fast."

"Luce, seriously..."

"Very serious, not just you, American eat too fast, block energy."

"That's what you're going to tell me?"

"Lucy not alway know."

"Really?"

"Can't alway spend mind on future, even Lucy have to live now. You want know where you end, Michael, but end do you no good, it end."

"I don't even know what to ask then."

"You need know step, first step and step after. Step become path."

"So this is my path? Eating Szechwan shrimp in a Chinese restaurant."

"Sometime path worn, many step before you, easy to find way. Sometime path not worn, not alway sure where step next. You different life, Michael, you not have ordinary life, you path not made."

"So what do I do?"

"Map no good if you not know where you are."

"I know where I am. I don't seem to know how to be anywhere else."

"Sometime easier to know where you not want to be than where you want to be. That okay, not have to alway know where you go."

"Good, 'cause I don't have a clue where I'm going…I never did, my life just sort of happened and then I met Kelli and everything was about her…without her, I don't know, I'm just sort of…waiting."

"What you wait for?"

"I don't know, maybe for like a…sign or something."

"River best when it move, water stay clear, fish happy."

"Yeah okay, so what do I do then?"

"You like river water, best keep moving, you find you way."

"You think?"

"Go eat, chew forty time, that good step now, everything follow."

**AIM FOR THE STARS
BUT WATCH YOUR STEP**

PEKING NOODLE CO.

Our births are marked by signs, by elements and Chinese years, our luck's in line with a moment of stars, with trite decisions that put us to the path and chance collisions we couldn't walk away from. It's hard to know what matters in a life, what these old world women have a way of seeing, what they trace together to the planets and to the lines in our hands, your fortune for $50, four yes or no questions for another $25. But there's a Quiznos where the Hungarian lady mystic used to be and the stars all seem to come and go these days, what's there at night and gone by morning, so I wonder if I was just dreaming. Scientists say they're all just suns in some other place's day, what's as far away as God or a good intention, their light a million years old by the time we see it. I can't help but think they might have all blown out by now or gotten small and cold and what we see is only a sort of ghost, like we never got the real thing, what stars you can see from a city like this, what haven't gone black yet with the soot and the wood smoke.

"Hello."
"Michael dear, how are you?"

"…I'm okay…Ahh…how are you?"

"As cheeky as ever I'm afraid."

"Ahh…well…that's cool I guess…um…"

"You divvy bastard…you have no idea who this is, do you?"

"Um…"

"It's Chrissy, you monster."

"Chrissy Pritty?"

"I'm completely destroyed."

"Jesus Chrissy, gimme a break, it must be like…I don't know, four or five years or something."

"Nonsense I saw you at Clive's Grammy party last year, you were with that child bride of yours."

"Kelli?"

"We weren't introduced, though the rumor was a girl named Kelli was making you miserable, I'll assume from the looks on your faces that was her."

"Yeah, well, Clive's parties suck."

"I rather love them."

"You can have 'em and the rest of it for that matter, I'm done with the whole shitty business."

"I heard you're not at Epic anymore."

"Yeah? who told you that?"

"I ran into Peter in New York, he said I should ring you when I'm in L.A.."

"Speaking of the whole shitty business, what's Peter up to?"

"He's still with that cheerless woman…"

"Helena?"

"She's beastly."

"Come on, she's…I don't know…she's just…German."

"Exactly, I couldn't have said it better."

"I don't even know who he's handling now."

"He's managing some hottest new thing in the UK."

"Who?"

It's all the same bollocks, something about someone's panties, Molly's britches or some sort of rubbish."

"Peter always had a knack for the cutting edge shit."

"He's a bit barmy, but you can't help but love him."

"Yeah, he's a good guy…so whattya doin' with yourself these days?"

"I'm still repping for Pop Sound."

"I have to admit sometimes I really miss the music, the business I couldn't give a shit about, but the music…I miss."

"It's hardly music and there's barely any business left."

"It's a different world for sure, these kids don't even know what a cd is, the big record company days are pretty much over I guess."

"You know I'm in town with one of our bands until Wednesday and…well Peter tells me you're on your tod these days and I was thinking…"

"On my what?"

"On your tod, dear, on your own. Peter said that you could use some company."

"Peter's a fucking idiot."

"He's a bit daft, but he's a good bloke."

"I know he thinks he's helping me, I'll give him this, he's the only person that's bothered to call me since everything went down at Epic, but I'm fine."

"I think he's afraid you're becoming a hermit up there on that mountain all by yourself."

"We're just separated, Kelli and me…we're working on things, you know, I don't need any sympathy."

"Well good, because I'm in dire straights…it's me birthday today, which is bad enough, and my plans have gone completely pear shaped."

"You know I love the accent and all, Chrissy, but I never know what the hell you're talking about."

"Accent? It is called English you know."

"Well pear shaped is the way we'd describe some lady's ass in Indianapolis."

"…it's like o.m.g. a complete disaster, then. Is that better?"

"Totally."

"Seriously Michael, I'm stuck in this naf hotel in Hollywood, I was supposed to be back in London, well I won't go on about it, it's all too tragic. But, I was thinking maybe my old mate might come to my gallant rescue."

"Chrissy, I can't do the whole birthday party thing…"

"Good God, it's the last thing I want, I've already had enough birthdays, thank you. I was thinking though, well, the telly was saying that there's to be a meteor shower tonight, a once in a lifetime type of thing, you know, and Peter tells me you have this beautiful mountain house and I thought it's been too long since I've seen Michael…or a meteor shower for that matter…"

"Chrissy, it's…it's kind of a bad time right now."

"You mean with these beastly fires? They seem far enough away, though you could smell the bloody smoke all the way in Hollywood."

"Well actually…I mean, there's hardly any furniture

here...I'm planning on selling the house and the Realtor says the house shows better empty and..."

"All I fancy is a nice glass of wine with an old mate and a quick gander at a few falling stars. We don't really need any furniture, I mean you can't watch the stars from inside the house now, can you?"

"Um...I guess not, but..."

"Perfect then, now how does one get there?"

"Well, um...I guess from Hollywood your best bet is..."

"I'm already on the main road."

"Which main road?"

"Topanga, dear."

"You're in Topanga?"

"I'm at that cute little liquor store on the main road."

"Why would you be in Topanga?"

"It's a long, boring story, I'll tell you over a drink, so what should I bring up?"

"You know Chrissy...I don't really drink anymore, I..."

"Michael darling, it's me birthday, do have a little fun, this nice gentleman is waiting for me to decide."

"I don't know, wine I guess?"

"Red or white, darling?"

"Um, red?"

"Michael, it's so bloody hot, how about a nice chilly white?"

"That's fine, I don't..."

"Brilliant ! Two of those..."

"I'm not going to drink that much, I..."

"Hold on Michael...yes, yes...Michael dear, why don't

you tell this nice chap here at the liquor store where you live and he can perhaps draw me a little map, it's a bit dodgy with it getting dark and all...here now hold on...yes, yes...he's going to tell you...if you can just draw that out for me..."

She called herself Welsh, a kind of good witch, but not so good she wouldn't push you over her spell, a sort of broken down angel, beguiled and bedeviled, old bed springs and walk away car wrecks. She was something once and no one now, nothing more than a story that always ends with then. She fronted one of those one hit bands in the eighties, Brit new wave pop, pink hair and an MYV video. But everything would turn sort of punk again and angry, everything was Nirvana and Pearl Jam, grunge bands soaked thru and sad with Seattle rain...and she seemed just under an umbrella.

She was green eyed and blonde legged, legs too long to sit proper, legs that were meant solely for sex. Everyone around her wanted her and I strangely didn't. It's what I told myself, it's what it took to take her, a wide eyed disinterest, if I'd known. But it's the kind of regret men keep and finger thru in their top dresser drawers, what we could have done and didn't. And everything we did that we wish we hadn't is the fiber of our youths, the mud our lives are built from and the sure trick of time and experience that it is anything less.

I look around trying to remember where I am, what seems more important than who I am and what I was once. The house is old and bone, stripped to its skin, to its milk paint, lath and plaster rock, Douglas fir subfloors refinished to an old idea. Everything is in boxes, "in transition," what Hannelore says instead of dead and gone. It reminds me of the weeks after my mother died. Her things on the spare bedroom bed like an evening wake, but she was Irish and the Irish watch over their dead for days. It hits me that we are dead, Kelli and me, the house and the hope we had. The story of us I'll keep in the boxes and never really unpack. And some day on a particular day and date, I'll take them to the Salvation Army and leave another piece of me behind and finally be small enough, maybe, to be a man.

"Michael! It's brilliant!"

"Hey Chrissy, I'll be right down. Come on in! I'm sorry things aren't a little more…hospitable."

"Rubbish, look at this place, now I know why you're living like a hermit up here, who'd ever leave, it's a paradise…she must be mad."

"Maybe it was the company."

"She's just young, she'll be back."

"She wasn't that young."

"Bollocks, she's a baby, let her get a little taste of the wankers out there. Believe me, she'll come running back."

"Did you ever go back?"

"Go back to what? Love?"

"Yeah, to someone you left…"

"I was daft, I'm sure Miles told you as much, you two were mates."

"The problem with Miles is half of everything he says is complete bullshit and the other half is the absolute truth, so you never know what to believe."

"I've lost my wits over a bloke or two, if that's what you're asking."

"I think women move on, when they leave they're already gone...men...I don't know, we just plod along in the same little circle."

"I need a drink for this conversation, be a love and open us a bottle."

"White or white?"

"White and put an ice cube in, please."

"I didn't know you were such a connoisseur."

"Oh naff off, it's me birthday now, be a gentleman and meet a lady's simple request."

"You're absolutely right...my apologies."

"You know you're looking quite fit, Michael. It's really not fair, you blokes just keep getting more and more dashing and well, let's just say old Chrissy ain't what she used to be."

She is thinner in her face, creased close to her eyes if you look, skin that was genius, what has become merely common sense. She is straight up still as if her body remembers. She remembers. She is the sum of things her youth can't forget or add up to and lived in like a grand house, like something that could never be built again. She is beautiful, but I won't tell her, what the worst and the best part of me won't let me say.

"Here you go, white wine, one ice cube."

"Brilliant, cheers."

"Cheers, happy birthday."

"For God's sake, get yourself a glass, it's bad luck to drink alone, and on me birthday no less."

"You know...I...I don't really drink anymore."

"No one's saying you have to get bladdered."

"I'm just trying to...I don't know, you know...be clean, or get clean..."

"You can have a glass of wine with your old mate, Chrissy, can't you? For my birthday? You can go straight back to being a monk or whatever it is that you're doing up here tomorrow. The idea that you Los Angelenos are all so free spirited is pants, you're such a blinkered bunch, you are."

"All right, fine...here, I've got a glass, I don't want to be accused of being...blankered."

"Blinkered. And you're a dear, now we can toast proper...to old friends."

"To old friends."

"This place really is brilliant. You're a jammy one, you are, you always have been, luck of the Irish I expect."

"I don't know, I'm wondering lately if my luck hasn't run up."

"Michael, you were a security bloke at the Roxy, and then Axel, right?"

"Yeah."

"And you wound up a VP at Epic, for God's sake. Mate, have a butchers around, you're the jammiest bastard I know."

"Hey, I've been busting my ass my whole life."

"Not to say you don't deserve it, but there's lots of poor buggers out there that deserve it, working their goolies off and never showing a bloody thing for it."

I can't say I knew what I wanted, I think we can't ever know where we're headed or what we really need. How

I got here is the long story, what I wear like a t-shirt tan and a scar above my left eye. I didn't know the way or the wind, the Santa Anas blow east to west, I just knew I had to keep moving.

"Michael, should we sit outside then?"

"Yeah, uhm, hold on, I have to clean off the chaise cushions…sorry, I don't think they've been touched since spring. I don't even know why I put them out."

"I could live out here, though I have to say these Santa something or other's…"

"Santa Anas."

"Precisely, yes, they are a bit overwhelming. Stone me! Did you see that? Bloody brilliant!

"Jesus, that was amazing. I've never seen anything like that.

"Cheers Michael, cheers, if there isn't another tonight that was the best prezzie I…oh!

"Christ, that had to hit, it looked like it landed just over the mountain.

"Can you imagine? You're some everyday bloke sitting at the homestead, watching the telly and a meteor crashes thru the roof. I mean what would you do?"

"It depends what I was watching."

"I wonder…has that happened?"

"Everything's happened."

"Bloody hell."

"Michael, do you have regrets?"

"About what?"

"What if that meteor crashed down right here on the house, would you regret…not doing something that you wished you had?"

"It's hard to say you regret not doing something, you know?"

"Not really, love?"

"I mean, how do you know what you could have done and what would come of it? It's just a fantasy. It's the things that I've done that I regret."

"You were always a thinker, Michael, even back in the days when you were a blokey bloke bouncer type."

"Oh yeah, it takes a real intellect to carry someone off stage by their collar."

"Bollocks, the lot of us would be carrying on in the dressing rooms, getting pissed out of our minds, and there you'd be, brooding about, always so serious."

"I probably just didn't know what to say."

"You knew what not to say, It's quite becoming, you know. All that strong silent type bollocks…it drives us birds barmy."

A quiet is what I know, what I own or what owns me, what seems to beat out from my chest. Even the canyon traffic and the early morning waves don't seem to matter, not enough to make their way in the windows and drown out this gristle of alone. I had it as a kid like some childhood condition they thought I'd out grow, coming home from school, my mother boxed and buried, the old man at work til six, the tin of the t.v. to keep me company, Gilligan's Island and the Bradys.

"Where you off to?"

"What?"

"You were off thinking about something…and I'm blabbering away like an old crow to myself."

"Sorry."

"Should we open the other bottle?"

"Jesus, we went thru that bottle already?"

"It's just some white wine, Michael, really."

"Are you going to be all right to drive?"

"Getting rid of me already?"

"No…I just…well these roads are tricky up here, especially if you don't know them and you do drive on the other side of the road back home."

"One more for the proverbial old road, Michael dear, and I'll be out of your hair. I don't want to be a bother."

"Come on, I didn't mean it that way."

"Cheers, Michael, cheers. Really, it's all right, love. I'm chuffed to bits, I just wanted to see some stars for me birthday."

"This is all kind of…weird for me, you know?"

"What's weird?"

"Being here in the house with you and everything the way it is right now…I…I don't know…I…"

"It's just two old mates having a laugh, nothing complicated."

"Maybe Peter's right, maybe I am turning into a hermit."

"You've been a perfect host and a perfect gentleman."

"Come on Chrissy, I'm a fucking disaster."

"You've been perfect, really, maybe too perfect…bloody hell!"

"Jesus…"

A meteor tears thru the pitch, a night hung up above us as if there was a light behind all this all along, an instance of God or good luck, some bit of matter burning in the rich air. And just as quick, a universe of black closes in around it so it is only a spectacular moment after thirteen billion years of a kind of life. It is the price of chance, everything is all or nothing. It is intimate if not impossible, as if I should have looked away. A gone by universe, a glance of skin, a shadow or the black silk of her panties, the purposeful push of her dress back over her white thighs and maybe a splinter of hesitation, a sort of promise I couldn't quite hear. And everything is only the wind again.

"Michael, why do you think we never slept together?"

"Uhm, maybe because I was a friggin' bodyguard and you were dating David Bowie."

"I never really 'dated' Davey."

"I was being polite."

"Thank you...you've always been a gentleman with me."

"I never had a choice."

"You did, actually"

"What?"

"Have a choice...I always fancied you."

"Come on, you never looked twice at me."

"I did, you never took a butchers back."

"You're being nice, not that I mind, my ego has taken a bit of a pounding lately, but come on, you having your eye on me back in the day is a load of crap."

"It's true. You may think that times are hard for me now, post rock stardom and all, but times were harder back then. It was a lot for a twenty year old to...suss thru."

"Please, you were a force...you still are. I've been around enough rock stars to know...I don't know what that thing is exactly, but you had it, you still do."

"Now that's a load of crap. I was a one hit wonder, nothing more, an ordinary bird...and a barmy one at that."

There's nothing more for us to say, it seems we've said all we could ever say to each other without lying or telling the truth. The sky has stopped, I wonder now if there are any stars left. Everything here, even the sky, is always moving, airplanes and satellites, the stars all lining up and falling behind the mountain into the glow of the late Hollywood traffic. The air is elemental, animal all put together and spirit, what brings life to the trees and breaks their branches. But religion is like that and even God is consequent to barometric pressures, to high desert temperature shifts and the lack of humidity. The only answer is the weather.

She asks me something.

"What?"

Her words winnow and scatter under my feet, under the chaise and across the flat stones. Everything is one thing now, in these Santa Anas, paper litter and bougainvillea bract, the leaves like tiny dreams of a time of rain, all of us gone by and blowing from east to west. Her eyes are on me like hands. I pretend mine are on my glass and not across the line of her body, her dress a bit of trivia, a puzzle with all the pieces put back in place. My arms and legs are heavy with blood, with the heat, with the weight of the winds breathing only out. She moves across her chaise and onto mine, straddling my legs. She is between time, everything can only move before her or after her. The heat of her skin, of her hopelessly complex sex, burn thru my jeans onto my every nerve, the string of instinct from then to now, the irony of taut and the infinite softness we forever seek. Her mouth is on mine, it seems all I can see is black, though I don't know if my eyes are opened or closed. Her tongue is full, strange, direct. My body is a million years in the making, a single sight of blood, of bone, of muscle twitch and memory. I will follow, it's what men do, everything is a matter of physics, momentums before and after a collision. But a man's heart has a mass and a velocity of its own. What we can only measure after it's too late.

**LADY LUCK IS AT
YOUR SIDE**

PEKING NOODLE CO.

Every number knows a kind of luck and there's a luck in numbers, your chances are better the more swings you take, more is better than less. Everything these days has an answer, a science and a statistical probability, a psychology for what the math can't add up. Even the invisible is somehow seen, micron microscopes and carbon dating, X-rays and CAT scans, MRIs and genetic genomics. They know who we are now to our white cell counts, where we've been from our skin and hair, finger nails and spit. Every bit and piece of a life spread out like a field of seeds from one flower. Mystery is a failure, when it was magic before, when it was God. I don't have to guess, as luck would have it, I know what happened. But knowing is always of the past, wisdom is knowing the numbers before you roll.

"Michael...you look like you have the weight of the world on your shoulders....What's going on up at the house?"

"The same old thing."

"Are the fires not close to you?"

"They haven't evacuated us out yet. I think most of

my neighbors are gone, at least from the looks of it, but the old timers seem to all be staying put. It's kind of nice, actually, there's no traffic and you can park on the road."

"They haven't closed your canyon?"

"No, I had a…an old friend…come up to the house last night."

"That sounds nice."

"It kind of went pear shaped, actually."

"I'm not sure what you mean?"

"I should have known…um…it kind of went bad."

"Really, how so?"

"Things sort of spiraled out of control."

"Did you argue?"

"No…sort of the opposite."

"Oh. This was a female friend?"

"Yeah."

"Well, let's start with what happened, we can work on the why's after that."

"You sound like my friend, Lucy."

"Is Lucy your…'friend' from last night?"

"No, no, Lucy's not even a woman…I mean…well…I mean she is, kind of, actually…I don't know."

"Have we talked about Lucy? I don't think I have her in my notes."

"Probably not."

"How do you know Lucy?"

"She owns the Chinese place that I've been going to for like…God…since I've been in L.A.…like thirty years or something."

"Nothing romantic?"

"No, she was a man, I mean she might have all her, his…stuff, like you know, guy stuff."

"But you have a relationship with…let's just say "her" for the sake of simplicity."

"Yeah, we always talk, she's like a psychic or something, but for real, not like some boardwalk bullshit. She's really, I don't know, she's like you, I mean she's really smart about things."

"Michael, I'm no fortune teller, all I know of the future is that we're bound to our pasts until we break free and can be in the moment."

"That's what I mean, smart stuff like that."

"What does Lucy have to say about Kelli?"

"Lucy doesn't seem to know a lot about women, she can…see your death if she looks into your eyes, if you're a man. She could see her own death whenever she looked in the mirror, so, well he could, so he changed to a her, so she wouldn't have to see it, but that's before I knew her, him…it's a long story…"

"It's Los Angeles, everyone here's a long story."

"Yeah, I guess."

"So Lucy knows how and when you're going to die?"

"Yeah, but she won't tell me."

"That's probably a good thing."

"I know it all sounds crazy, but Lucy's like the real thing, it goes back fifty generations or something."

"Michael, there's a lot of things out there that have no explanation. I try to keep an open mind. For the sake of time though, let's get back to your friend from last night."

"Chrissy?"

"What's her name?"

"Chrissy…Chrissy Pritty."

"Chrissy...pretty?"

"Yeah, I know."

"That's quite a name."

"I think it's her real name, believe it or not."

"Do I know who this person is? That name sounds familiar."

"You might, I suppose Chrissy was kind of famous."

"Is she one of your musicians?"

"No, I knew Chrissy back when I was bodyguarding, like late eighties or something."

"I came to the U.S. in...'82."

"She sort of had her moment at the end of the new wave thing, like '87 maybe."

"Oh! I remember...mmmm, da, da, da, da, mmmm, da, da, mmmm, da, da, da, da...that's her, no?"

"That's it."

"Oh, I loved that song."

"You and like a couple of million other people."

"Sorry. We should keep things moving, I did love that song, though. So how does...um, Miss Pretty make her way up that mountain of yours? So to speak."

"I was just hanging out at home, you know, I mean, I wasn't out looking to get laid or anything."

"Michael, you and Kelli are separated, any promise between you is...on hold right now, you don't owe her fidelity at this point. You may owe it to yourself, but we'll get into that later.... So how did Miss Pretty find herself in Topanga?"

There's ten thousand sides to the story and a truth we never seem to land on. There's a gap under the front door where the wind blows in, where the whole world seemed to slip thru one day, the houses here are like that. The houses in Cleveland all had weather stripping and aluminum storm doors and ours with plastic sheeting over the windows in winter, what the old man put up so we could hardly see out 'til late spring when he took it off, but then it was all a blur anyway.

There can only be something where there was nothing before. What the book Kelli left on the nightstand on her side of the bed says, at least that's what it seems to say. It seems there's nothing left for me or for the hollowness that always fills in behind me. The house is packed up and attic ached and crawl spaced, the old paint peeled away. My shirts are too big, this city is too small so there's nowhere I can go now that I don't think of her. There are things that are too big for there to be anything after. Sometimes there can be only space.

"It's understandable...when Kelli moved out she left a hole in your life. That vacancy, is intense...it's going to take time to fill that in again. You will."

"I can't imagine...being with someone else."

"You haven't healed yet, someone like Chrissy is just going to make that void look even bigger."

"I feel more alone now than before, Hannelore. I don't know...how..."

"Everything changes, Michael, sometimes in just a moment."

The universe is expanding at 46 miles per second, the stars farther away every instant, the space between things growing further and further apart. Even the things that seem the same are different, the sun and moon, her and me, the distance of our hearts in light years now instead of just breaths.

"You were aware that your mother was sick, no?"

"Yeah, she was in and out of the hospital as long as I could remember, and in bed a lot of the time when she was home."

"Your needs as a child weren't being met."

"The old man did the best he could, I guess."

"Despite your father's best efforts you were pretty much left on your own. It developed a fierce independence and a resiliency about you, which is admirable, but there's still a part of you searching for someone. Kelli was bound to be attractive to you, but once the two of you got past the first six months or so, all the real...stuff...started to come out and, unfortunately, it did you in as a couple."

"It was that night at the Standard..."

"What's that?"

"That's when...when we sort of unraveled."

"Did we discuss this with Kelli?"

"We started to and then...well...I...that's the day I walked out."

"You did a little more than walk out, Michael."

"I'm so sorry, Hannelore. I'm..."

"You're absolutely forgiven, I told you that your first day back, but it's important that you acknowledge what happened."

"I feel like an idiot."

"You shouldn't, we've come a long way since then."

"It feels like a million years ago."

"It was."

"I really want to be a better person."

"You're finding your true self now, all that anger and such wasn't the real you, that was just your shield to protect yourself from any more hurt. It didn't work did it?"

"No."

Why don't you finish the story you started that day."

"About New York?"

"Please."

"I don't know what happened, I mean, like for sure, I know something happened, it's not anything I can put into words."

"You have good instincts, trust them."

"I don't know, it's like I felt something...break...I don't know how else to explain it."

"When you say the word 'break', what do you mean?"

"That's just it, I don't know, I just know something happened...we were in New York, I had to be there for an Andy Summers gig at Birdland and I thought I'd bring Kelli and make a sort of romantic week out of it..."

The city citied like it does, all belled and brindled, shout out and sang. Everything rang winter white and gray, every breath wrought out in the air from every mouth and manhole cover. And Kelli wrapped up in the cold like a Christmas present, like the cold was just for her, and me in my old boots and a broke down leather jacket and washed out jeans worn in and worn out. The streets were lit with street lights and people and stopped cars everywhere and buildings up into the air instead of trees, everything the genius of two hundred years of accidents and the math of eight million added up, the sudden calm of heavy glass doors and a terrazzo lobby and the rise of a boxed wood elevator, the formality of our room's reveal, our bags set in front of the bed like two virgins on their wedding night, the click close of the bellman backing out the door, and amongst all this it is only us again.

Kelli sat down on her side of the hotel bed like the white ironed sheet beneath her, perfectly, like anything that's spoiled the moment you use it as it's intended. I peeled her paper away like I had so many times before, her sweater in my undeserving hands, and only stopped when there was nothing left. I wasn't sure if she was gone or if it was me that had disappeared. Her eyes silent and mine screaming to be found. It was the end of something, of us, what she already knew and me going on with the two of us like we were one thing when we both knew we weren't even two, but nothing at all, an empty box no matter how beautifully it was wrapped.

"So there was nothing leading up to this that might explain Kelli's...detachment?"

"No."

"When you say, 'romantic weekend,' what did you expect?"

"I don't know...romantic."

"Did you want to have sex when you got to your room?"

"Well yeah, I mean, I...it didn't need to be, you know, sex, I don't know how to say it."

"Affectionate?"

"Yeah, affectionate."

"You had an expectation, not necessarily anything unrealistic, a young couple in love on a trip to New York."

"I guess so."

"Kelli's emotional state, whatever it was, was something you didn't expect and it triggered you...given your childhood's uncertainties, it's understandable."

"I don't like secrets, if that's what you mean."

"Your survival instincts are...over developed, it's part of what made you a good bodyguard, you're constantly reading the situation, interpreting details most people would never notice."

"I've always felt like I'm not really a part of things, like I'm on the outside looking in."

"Every time your mother left the house you weren't sure if you'd ever see her again so you developed a strong...intuition. If you knew what was going to happen, even if you couldn't dictate the outcome, it gave you some sense of control."

"I don't know what happened with Kelli."

"Actually you probably do...I don't doubt for minute that you were sensing something. Without over interpreting it, what do you think happened?"

"She fell out of love with me."

"Sort of like your mother just died one day?"

"Maybe."

"What do you believe about love?"

"I don't know if I can even say what love is...but whatever it is it doesn't seem to last."

"My best guess is you're convinced everyone you love, one way or another, will leave you."

"Yeah, probably."

"From the women you choose to be in relationships with to your behavior, you're working to support that belief."

"So I'm doing this to myself?"

"To a certain degree, yes."

"That's hard to hear."

"You're not in these relationships alone. Kelli picked you to support her beliefs. Kelli has a wounded bird quality about her, probably like your mother I expect. That's what you were attracted to, a chance to save her like you couldn't save your mother. And you, you were this archetype masculine figure that Kelli needed. You were perfectly right and wrong for each other, like a perfect storm."

I can feel the press of these pasts, my past and theirs, a pall of planets and the pull of the earth and time, the gravity of a life, mine and Kelli's, the old man's and my mother's, my mother's life like all she ever did was die. It is the centripetal grasp of it all, the second glances and her and her and me. I am between any hope of a heaven, of a plain forgiveness, and the hell of a forever where I'm picking at my scabs. The past is the pavement you're standing on, what can get you somewhere or leave you nowhere and peel your skin off when you fall, the now a curve in the road where you can only see where you've been, where you can't see ahead less you keep moving.

"What does Chrissy mean to you?"

"She doesn't mean anything to me."

"Well, you described her as a friend. Are you friends?"

"I did security for her boyfriend, it's not like we were hanging out."

"So when you and Kelli broke up she's not someone you called."

"God no."

"So maybe acquaintances is a better description?"

"Yeah, I mean she's cool, but...yeah, she's just some-one I knew back in the days."

"I have to think Chrissy is a pretty determined indi-vidual, no pun intended. A beautiful rock star..."

"That was a long time ago."

"I assume she's an attractive woman still."

"Oh yeah, maybe even better looking, actually."

"It's reasonable to say her ego was in a pretty, I can't stop saying that, sorry, a fairly perilous position. It was her birthday, which is hard enough for a woman, but she's also had a taste of fame...you might have been the first man to ever refuse her?"

"Believe me, no one says no to that...I must be crazy."

"No, you're in love with Kelli."

"I don't know what I am."

"I think you do. Your ego doesn't need superficial reinforcement. You're in a vulnerable place right now and you stayed within yourself, you've really made great progress."

"I thought you said no judgments?"

"It doesn't make you a bad person for having sex or a good person for abstaining, it's about making decisions that are emotionally healthy. You used a new set of emo-tional tools to be mindful rather than reactive."

"Yeah, but the old tool was a lot more fun..."

"You'll still have plenty of time to express your rogue self, don't worry.

"Michael, I think it's time for you to reach out to Kel-li...it's time to find out where you stand."

"Oh Jesus…do you really think I'm ready for that?"

"Yes, I do."

"Maybe we should do some more work?"

"The surest way to the cure is the cause."

"The last time I went over there it was a disaster."

"I think a letter would be best for now, something tactile, no email message or instant text thing, there's something lightweight about them."

"So what do I say?"

"Write out the things that you want Kelli to know, tell her what you tell me, we can work on a letter together next session if you want. Put somethings on paper, I think you'll be surprised what will come out."

"I don't know where to start."

"Start with your heart, Michael. That's all anyone could ask for."

SHORTEST WAY TO ANOTHER
HEART IS THRU YOU HEART

PEKING NOODLE CO.

"Hey Lucy...how's it going?"

She is beautiful, if I didn't know, and still maybe more beautiful because I do, Los Angeles will do that to you, so you're always sort of believing. This place will make you and jade you and bring you down with hope, this west will blind you with a sun and open your eyes to another way, another chance, like all your dreaming was a religion to pray to. We are everyone and everyone is a piece in this, the highways and the hills and this brief bit of infinity, this strip mall sprawl that stands as a city. I'm not from here, but it seems I'm from here now, tattooed and tanned and tattered at the ends like my old Vanson jacket, a hole in the right hand pocket, but the zippers still work.

"Michael, where you been? Not see you for a while."
"Yeah...I've been kind of laying low the last couple days."
"How you house?"
"It hasn't burned yet..."
"Tony say fire near you house."
"It's a couple of canyons over."

"Pictures on t.v. very bad."

"What's up with that, Luce? You're watching t.v. now?"

"Not watch, too many face, Tony show t.v. when picture of fire."

"It's weird, there's barely any smoke in Topanga, it's all going straight out over the ocean."

"People and nature no balance, painful when no balance."

"All that smoke sure makes for a pretty sunset though."

"Four people die."

"Yeah, I'm just talking shit, Luce…it's gallows humor, believe me, I'm just waiting for the flames to come up over the hill any time now."

"Lucy not know, what this gallow humor?"

"It's like making a joke out of serious stuff, it's sort of a western thing, I guess, you know, laughing about things you can't deal with."

"Need deal with thing."

"I suppose."

"When you deal with thing?"

"Whatta ya mean?"

"You know what Lucy mean."

"What? Kelli?"

"Need deal with Kellee."

"I've got you Lucy, we're working thru it, right?"

"No more gallow humor."

"I'm trying, you know, I'm seeing this therapist, Kelli and me were seeing her, you know, together, before we broke-up."

"Maybe need different person, not work first time."

"That was my fault, I walked out and…well anyway, I think she's helping me…you know, deal with things."

"You not deal with big thing. Need say truth."

"Come on Luce, you know me, I'm a lot of things, but I'm no liar."

"Need say truth to self."

"I know the truth all too well."

"What about therapis? She know truth?"

"Hannelore? I can't say I always know exactly what I'm feeling all the time or…you know, how to put things in words and stuff, but I've never lied to her…or anyone."

"You not say all of truth."

"Lucy, what are you getting at?"

"You keep piece of truth quiet, what you not say lie as much as not truth."

"So…what do you want me to say?"

"Need say Kellee dead."

I can only look straight into Lucy's eyes, I don't want her to see me alive. I'm instantly raging like a bad sun, like the fires in the hills, what I'm afraid to let out or I might burn the county down. I am what I could never put a name to or spit out, a history of violence, of bile, of hate, what's eaten my life away and turned my knuckles black.

A man and a woman and two children happen in the Lucky's door as the word 'dead' turns the air into ash, a fate or the simple trap of chance, the street noise around them and the wind, the smell of smoke like a family secret everyone in the neighborhood knows. The glass door squeezes closed like a hand closed around our throats, the sort of silence that inevitably follows such things, the awkward in between, what now could possibly be said? The man, an Asian man, with trivial hands and a desk job chin, takes the two children by the shoulders and steers them around and out the door. The woman steps next to me to ask for a table, she doesn't get it, she probably never does, but this is between men, anyway, what even Lucy can't hide below an inch of blue eye shadow, red lipstick, black liner and mascara.

"We need a…"
"We closed."
"The sign says 'open.'"
"Sign wrong."
"But it's seven o'clock, how can you be closed?"
"No food."
"Those people are eating."
"Kitchen no work, you need come back later, wait outside. Tony!"
"But…"

Tony appears like a good bar trick and gently moves the woman towards the door leaving a cart of dirty dishes where they were, what reminds me that even this day is, for someone else, an everyday. The woman teeters away, her hand digging at the bottom clutter of her purse, purposeless and nervous habit, skittish stutter, bargain store muttering, Tony smiling with only his teeth so I know he doesn't understand what she's saying. Her head turning from side to side as she talks and walks towards the door, looking into the dining room, looking in thru the big fish tank in the wall, the long fish letting her see the side of his eye for a second and then his languid turn and turn and turn again, so I don't know what any of us are doing here. I look back to Lucy. I'm choked, I can either whisper or scream, there seems no in betweens anymore. I swallow hard and talk thru my teeth.

"Have you known all along?"

"Lucy know."

"Why'd you let me go on acting like she was alive?"

"Time for every thing."

"Did you know she was going to die?"

"Everyone die."

"I mean did you know when! Did you know when she was going to die?"

"Everyone know that to. She know, you know."

"What the fuck are you talking about?"

"Kellee have death all round her, that why she so beautiful."

"Lucy, I'm serious, no more bullshit…"

"Lucy serious too."

"Why didn't you tell me?"

"No good to know, tell you and you life become death."

"But we're friends, Luce. You…you could have stopped her…Fuck…you could of stopped me."

Lucy is looking into my eyes, I won't look away. I wonder what death she sees, what life I have left, a lifetime pouring down my face, all of it a fate I'm not sure I didn't choose, what I couldn't cry out until now. I don't need to tell her what happened, she knows what happened.

The Highway Patrol on the phone, a wide-hipped cop at a concrete block station, a click clack metal desk, three hours of grief training under his elbows. I don't remember his name, I remember his timbre and the word 'accident,' the words 'yes I'm her husband' coming out from my mouth, the sound of saying husband thin in my throat, a sort of panic that he'd find me out, that he'd know I couldn't feel a thing, water coming out of the kitchen faucet, what I calmly turned off, a well of dark blood spreading out from my heart to my hands and feet where it all turns blue and returns again, an address where I would need to pick up her things, there's no need to identify the body, words I'm not sure he said, but what I understood, what I might of heard in a movie instead, a scrap of paper and a cheap pen, a pen I had to scratch back and forth to make work, an address somewhere on Mission Road somehow off the 5.

I hung up the phone and sat down in a kitchen chair, her chair, where she sat, the scrap of paper in my hand, thinking back to when she first gave me her number, what she wrote on the back of a fortune cookie fortune. I sat there for days, for years, five minutes by the clock, but time is a lie like that. I thought to scream and yell, to put my fist through the wall, but I couldn't be angry at her anymore, all I could do was love her. Love is love's revenge. All I could do was wait, for what I don't know, the sound of the refrigerator keeping me from spinning off the earth. It is the singular moment a life adds up to, the news of a death, something so pure you see right thru it and nothing around it, and for just that moment the nothingness that a life is. I remember looking at my hand hanging up the phone as if it wasn't mine, but something miles from here, tracing a mark around my finger where my ring had been, what I'd left in Hannelore's office the afternoon I'd walked away. I remember wondering what happened to it, what I thought of just then and not before. The Highway Patrol had called the house from the information on Kelli's driver's license, she hadn't changed her license or registration. It's what I hold onto now, as if it was some way of her saying she still loved me. It's the last thing about her that was mine.

I've just now realized I'm in the kitchen with Lucy, the Lucky's staff waiting outside the swinging doors, standing in their old shoes, wishing they could smoke. The kitchen air is thick with work, with sixty years of fry oil and today's fish, everything almost acrid and a comfort still.

"Lucy, when you see someone's...death...do you see it like you're watching it or do you see it like...um, like they're going to see it?"

"Don't know."

"Whataya mean? You don't know?"

"Not know where spirit go, you maybe see you own death same way Lucy see."

"Did you...see Kelli die?"

"Not see into woman eye. Woman a mystery."

"I...I hope she wasn't...scared, you know?"

"Spirit know it way, how die natural to the way, dying easy, living hard thing."

"I fucked it all up, Luce."

"Life go it own way, Michael, not see everything at once, but it right way in end. You be okay, you see."

"I guess so."

"No guess, that truth. All go same way in end."

"Yeah, Luce, I know, we're all going to die, but…what we do, you know, with our lives…matters…right?"

"No control everything. Same soil, same water, some time good rice, some time bad rice, in end both rice fill you belly."

"Speaking of rice, I've kept you long enough, you can't shut down the restaurant because of me, I feel like an idiot."

"It okay, you good friend to Lucy and to Lucky House."

"Luce, please…I'm going…you know, you've got a business to run."

"It okay, good for business."

"Come on, this is crazy, you can't keep all these people waiting."

"People want wait."

"No one wants to wait, Lucy."

"Every people want wait.

"Lucy, you're nuts…I'm getting out of here so you can get back to work."

"It okay, Michael, people stand in line, make thing special. Not want right away, no wait too easy, too easy no good."

"Is that why you don't seat people right away?"

"Now you know Lucy secret."

"I always wondered why there'd be people waiting in front when there were empty tables."

"It okay not tell every thing to people, but need tell every thing to self."

"Yeah…"

"Sit down, eat, you feel better."

"I don't feel much like eating, Lucy, I'm going home."

"You stay, you not drive now."

"Why?" What did you see?"

"Same thing alway see."

"So why don't you want me to drive home now?"

"You be hungry later, wish you eat."

"I think maybe you're not telling me the whole truth now."

"Lucy tell what need know."

"You can't change the future, right Luce? Everything is what it is."

"Sit down, eat shrimp, very fresh, black bean sauce, you feel better, then you drive."

"No, it's time to go. Thanks Lucy…"

"Michael, you not go now, you need listen, trust Lucy."

"I do trust you."

"You stay then, eat."

"No, you know better than anyone, Luce, you can't change your fate."

"Can't know what next, Michael."

"You know."

"Lucy know end, but every one know end, how you get there still mystery."

**EVEN A LONG LIFE IS
A SHORT LIFE IN THE END**

PEKING NOODLE CO

There was a bird on the front patio stones when I got home from the Lucky, what likely flew into the reflection of a blue sky in the window glass above, a congregation of ants coming and going away from it like there was almost nothing else, as if it was the last thing, the kind of thing I'd look back on and say that's when it all started or stopped, it's hard to know the difference now. It was a small bird like the bird before, what I killed when I was twelve and hid from the old man under a rock. I couldn't help, but to look in its greasy eye, wondering what Lucy would see, wondering if it were a ghost maybe, or some kind of sign. I could see the porch light in its shine and a sort of reflection of myself, the winds and the burnt black air around me. I left it at the door and went inside. Lucy was right, I'd go to bed hungry. The next morning there was nothing, no bird or even ants, like it all never happened.

It's hard to say where things come from and go to, it seems to me now that everything is some consequence of loss, of the nothing after, everything starts with some sort of end. I suppose something has to die so something else can live, heaven and hell are like that. Everything is always changing, aging, moving thru time, everyone in this city is driving all at once. There's talk of adding a lane to the 10, but it's probably just talk, it will take years if it ever happens. They say the universe is expanding every second, revolving around itself and pulling apart, the space between things growing bigger and bigger, what the city planners try their best to fill in. It seems everything is getting smaller and smaller, wearing away and breaking down into pieces, tatter carried away by an infinity, some invisible gravity of dark matter or ants, all of it becoming something else, something too big to see all at once.

"Hey dad."
"Hey Mikey, how's it going out there?"
"Okay."
"I've been watching the t.v. about those fires."
"Yeah, it's been pretty bad."
"So what are you going to do?"
"Wait it out, I guess."
"I can't see why they don't have them out by now, it's not like they're a surprise or something, it's been weeks or a month even."
"They're huge fires, dad. You can't just put them out."
"I'll never understand California..."
"Me neither.... So how are the Browns doing?"
"They almost won today, damn Bengals edged it out, but they got this kid from Texas at quarterback, I think he's going to be pretty good. Kind of reminds me of you, he's not the biggest guy on the field, but he's tough."

"Yeah, I could take a hit, I just couldn't throw the ball."

"Hell, you were as good as any of them ever come thru here, you didn't have any confidence, that's that damn Kryzinski's fault…he's still coaching, you know, I go to a game every now and then, he's as bad as ever, the guy doesn't know his ass from a hole in the ground."

"He's no genius, but you gotta give the guy a break, it's a thankless job."

"What about you? You find anything yet?"

"Dad, you don't find a whole lot of jobs like I had, they sort of find you."

"Yeah, you were the president, so how's the president get fired?"

"Vice President…of A and R, dad, there were plenty of stupid assholes above me."

"That's the problem with these non-union jobs. You got no job security."

"I was pretty lucky, they're still paying out my contract, this is my last month."

"A contract? I never did understand what you did over there."

"I baby sat a bunch of rock stars."

"So why can't you find some more rock stars to babysit?"

"There aren't any rock stars, dad…not anymore."

"That's the problem with this country, we just don't make anything anymore, God damn outsourcing, people are hurting everywhere, I guess."

"Yeah, it's weird times."

"You know I saw that Ruth girl's mom at the Fazio's, I didn't say anything. You ever see her?"

"No, that was a long time ago, dad. She moved back home I think..."

We lived at the beach, me and her, the first girl. We could only afford the Valley when we got here, but we faked it and drove an old shitty car that looked cool like we meant it, and stole enough from the door and the club's cut to make it. We'd come cross country with our t.v. ideas and a trunk full of clothes we wouldn't wear, a rust belt town soaked into our bones. We lived at the beach, so the sun never shined, most of the time the weather was no better than Cleveland. We snuck into a pad in Venice like we were stealing a car someone had already stole, the best parts stripped, everywhere were tripped out kids and old men ghosts scuffing their feet, walking out brown bottle hearts, everyone rags, on the skids, on the Strand, to the beat. But Abbott Kinney turned around with a new hip money scene, new t-shirts made to look old and two hundred dollar jeans. Santa Monica was newly painted with traffic ticket cash, the whole Westside like an older woman in a short skirt, something beautiful once and bordering on ridiculous with makeup and money now.

We broke into pieces, me and her, too small to hold onto or sift out of the sand, Los Angeles is like that, but cities die at their core and we never seemed to have a middle, as if we happened all at once. This place will die like a star, shining fast and furious across a nightless sky, young and burning beautiful before it can burn out, before anything can change, before it can turn old. And no one will believe it and everyone will say they saw it coming, another Mulholland Highway car crash, 3 am, a hundred miles per hour, what the Sheriff will figure from the skid marks, flowers and a small white cross where it all went down, burned out seven day candles at the curve it couldn't quite make. It's how we want it, stories are what we make here.

"Dad...do you think mom was happy?"

"Your mother? What do you mean?"

"I don't know, I've just been thinking about her lately and...I don't really have any memories of her happy."

"Mikey, your mom was pretty sick towards the end, but that wasn't her...that was just sort of the end of her. When she was pregnant and you were born, I don't think she could've been any happier. She loved you, Mikey...and she loved being a mom more than any-thing."

"Did you and mom fight?"

"Like everyone I guess, you get in little scuff ups, Mikey, anybody that you care about, but your mom and me, no, nothing that ever meant anything. I remember, before you were born, I was watching the Indians and your mother had dinner ready and I wasn't coming to the table, so she came and dumped my dinner right on my lap. I looked up at her and we both just busted out laughing...and let's face it, it wasn't much of a loss, your mother was a lot of things, but a good cook wasn't one of them."

"How'd you and mom meet?"

"I never told you that story?"

"If you did I don't remember..."

"Well, she was dating Ronny Urbanski, that's back when kids were proper Catholics and you just went to a movie or something, not like these younger generations having sex in the car and all."

"So that's how you met mom? On a date not having sex with Ronny Urbanski?"

"Well, I'm not finished."

"All right, go on, I'm just giving you a hard time."

"So, your mother went to Saint Joseph's, you know that, that was an all girls school in Rocky River, it was a part of town I'd never seen. Urbanski was back from college somewhere, I don't know where, probably some fancy east coast school. They were on a date and his car broke down, he was driving this European thing, a Karmann Ghia or some little something like I'd never seen before.... And that's how I met your mother."

"So how do you go from she's on a date with some college guy with a sports car to this is the woman you marry?"

"I was working after school at George's Sohio and knew a thing or two about cars, but this damn thing, it didn't even have a radiator, like a motorbike or something, the engine in the back, anyway, I got it started up eventually, but it was missing bad and it wasn't going to go far. I think Ronny was more worried about the car than his date...so I took her home to Rocky River."

"And...?"

"Well this might surprise you, but I was pretty cool back in the days."

"So you stole her away from the college guy?"

"Yeah. I guess so."

"Nice..."

"So...they catch the guy doing all this crap?"

"The fires? No. They don't know shit, they think he might drive a blue truck, that's all they got."

"People do strange things, I don't understand it."

"Yeah, yeah they do..."

It is a beginning, how the small man sees it, the end of everything before us, but he has the eyes of a believer and believers see what the rest of us are just looking for. He is what we made of him, what he made of himself, what the t.v. news makes of him now. He is the smell of medicine, of A & D Ointment and Aspirin, of washed hands with white soap. He makes sure to wash his hands with soap and hot water so it hurts, under his nails and up his arms to his elbows. He uses bleach for his t-shirts, for his underwear and his socks. He lives alone, but he puts the toilet seat down. He flushes twice when he pisses, three times for shits.

He will buy gas today where he always buys gas, in the Valley at the Arco for cash and cigarettes he won't smoke and a pack of matches please, por favor. He will fill up the truck and a five gallon can for a lugger and a roof cutter and a planer, maybe, or a weeder and a blower, a chain saw and a mower, He must have a reason, we'll never think twice, he works with his hands, his hat will tell you that. He will go to two buildings today, Santa Monica and the Palisades. He will take the canyon road home instead of the highway and listen to the am radio, to the weather and the traffic and the news of the fires.

He will eat a sandwich for dinner, it's too hot for the stove, white bread and ham and mustard and watch the local t.v. and wait for the in between of night and the very early morning. He will cut out a picture of the fire from the Times and put it with the others. He will strike a match and dream.

"So how's the weather?"

"Um…hot, with a hundred percent chance of ash…"

"You can come home till those fires get taken care of…if you want."

"Thanks dad, I know…I'm…hanging tight for now."

"Well, it can't stay hot forever, that's why it's weather, it's always something else tomorrow."

"Yeah…I guess…well I better get going."

"Yep."

"I'll talk to you next week, okay?"

"Yep, next week, hopefully I'll have better news, we're playing Buffalo next week."

"All right…well, take care dad, I love you."

"Love you too Mikey, be good."

"Ok dad, bye."

The mule deer and coyotes are coming into town, looking for food, for water, for an escape from the fires, from the smoke, awkward on the even asphalt, all of them with dull looks in their eyes where they shined in the car lights before. There are pilot whales washing onto the beach in Carlsbad without explanation, thirty-five so far, but nature is hap and chance, God and man a plan, what he giveth and what we taketh away. The old Santa Monica Greyhound bus station is gone, there's a Bank of America there now, but the Greyhound sign is still on the roof. The city council designated it a historical landmark, some last little bit of the old beach, something so we can know where it all started and where it stopped.

**WHEN YOU AT THE END
START SOMETHING NEW**

PEKING NOODLE CO

I know about God from my mother, from the nuns at Saint Basil's, from my father and his Jesus face. I know about God and believing, but it's luck I've lived on so far. There's ashes on the windowsills, on the truck, in each breath we take now, a certain cough we carry along these days, what we'll keep until they bury us or burn us down to what's left. It's a 118 degrees downtown, the hottest day ever recorded in Los Angeles. The news says it may be even hotter, that the national weather service thermometer at the Civic Center broke this morning, there's no telling when technicians will have it repaired. Until then we'll have to go with our guts, put a hand out the house and feel for the heat, trusting what we know, what ten thousand years have taught us, that all this must be the end of something.

"Michael, how are you?"
"I'm okay."
"This heat is really something…"
"Yeah."
"The radio said that it's the hottest day downtown since they've been keeping record."

"Yeah, I heard that."

"I suggested you write Kelli a letter, did you bring anything to go over?"

"No, I…uhhh…didn't write anything."

"Have you given any thought to what you might want to say?"

"I don't know what to say…"

"Michael, is everything okay?"

"Hannelore…I need to talk to you about something."

"Of course, that's why I'm here."

Once I say it, it'll be done, the spell cast and broken with the same word, Kelli forever in a sleep and me in this insomnia. Once I was dreaming, in this California, in this bird-egg blue, an ocean and always a sky, the pull of the moon and the tide of her long long hair. This is where we started, her and me, where we stopped short it seems. Los Angeles is the beginning and the end of everything, of a big America and our beat western dreams, the narrow road where we lived, what spills into the ocean at its end like a still pitch river. We couldn't have happened anywhere else, the two of us, but here. We couldn't have gone any further without getting wet. Luck is like that, a kind of faith in desperation, and love is no different than luck, it settles in some places more than others, like the cold fills in in the canyons until the sun, late mornings the next day.

"Hannelore…uhhh…Kelli…Kelli's dead."

"My God…Michael…how?"

"A car accident."

"I'm so sorry, it…I don't know what to say…Did you hear from her family?"

"No, the Highway Patrol called me, she hadn't changed the address on her Drivers License, it's weird, she was always so on everything like that, like thank you letters and extra keys and you know, all that kind of stuff."

"Michael, you can always reach me on my cell."

"I can't figure it out, why she didn't change it, I mean she wrote her maiden name on the mailbox at the apartment, I don't know, it doesn't make sense..."

"When were you notified?"

"I've known for a while."

"When my father passed away it felt like time stopped."

"You know...uhh, Hannelore, I know you're doing everything to help me and I uhhh...feel like these last weeks have made a huge difference in me...really...I want you to know that I really appreciate you taking me back, you know, and giving me another chance and everything...I...I know I didn't show you...the kind of respect you deserve...before, but I want to...I've changed, right?"

"Michael dear, slow down, it's okay, you've had a terrible shock, but I'm confused, you said you've known for a while, when did this happen?"

"It was a few months ago."

"So Kelli's been dead this entire time?"

"Yeah...I wanted to make things right, you know...so when I like...pack it in I'll be a good person, the person Kelli wanted me to be...that's all I was trying to do, I didn't mean to keep anything from you."

"I need a moment to process this...so when did Kelli die?"

"June 17th."

"And she died in a car accident?"

"On Topanga Canyon, I don't know what she was doing on the canyon at that time of night, it was late, like 2 am or something, that's what they think, the County Sheriff said she might have hit a deer, there was blood on the front bumper, but no deer."

"Do you think she was driving up to see you?"

"I don't know…it's been making me crazy trying to figure out what it all means, they think the car was going down, so if she was coming to see me, she changed her mind."

"It was late, she may have been missing you and wanted to drive by the house, sort of make a safe connection. It makes sense now, that's why she just stopped her therapy."

"Hannelore, did Kelli love me?"

"Michael, I…what Kelli discussed with me…I have to maintain that confidentiality, even now."

"I just hope she loved me, you know, even for just a minute. If she didn't, then I don't have anything."

"Michael, you've progressed past that line of thought, you know who you are, that's not defined by someone else."

"Hannelore, please."

"This is a difficult thing, I…do you think Kelli would have come to therapy with you if she didn't love you?"

"People probably do all kinds of things to avoid change."

"You definitely have learned something here. But Michael, seriously, you shouldn't think that I somehow know Kelli better than you."

"Please Hannelore…"

"Michael…I…oh, the hell with it. Yes, I believe Kelli used the word love in our discussions, but it's just a word, it's not real because I say it. It's real because you felt it. You have to trust yourself, that's the leap we all have to take to love…and to be loved."

Love is the best of us and somehow the worst of me, what makes the world perfect in the end, and ruined me with time. I drive now with the radio off, with the windows down, searching for some piece of her, for a breath she might have breathed in and out that night, what might have drifted down the canyon road to the beach and mixed in with the ocean air. The County finally replaced the guard rail in August, the skid marks have faded away with the wear of the traffic, commuters cutting thru Topanga from the Valley, so there's almost nothing left of her, old clothes in boxes in the closet at the house, what Maria Elena can't bring herself to take. Kelli's grandmother's credenza and a China cabinet waiting quietly, her purse and a large manila envelope, what the Sheriff labeled personal affects, what I haven't had the guts to open. The rest of it went with her to 500 California Street, what her mother took away, something less than an echo left at apartment eight, a couch and an IKEA kitchen table and chairs, a night stand, a mattress frame and a mattress.

I would never see her again, her at the coroner's like a small field flower that's too small to pick, what could only be saved pressed between two pages in a book. And still she was perfect or something even more than perfect, empty of anything, like dying stripped away all her leaves, like all that was left was the hush of a new snow across her branches, what fell while we were sleeping, everything in a Michigan Christmas moonlight that no one would see. She is dead. She will always be dead now, even in my memories she will be see thru and a sort of make believe. Her parents had her body brought back to Muskegon two days later and buried her before they could look. Kelli wanted to be cremated, but I didn't fight them, my final failure to her.

"Michael, it's essential to our work together that you be forthright with me."

"I've been honest about everything, even Kelli, except for her being dead."

"That's a pretty big exception."

"I know you're mad at me…"

"Michael, I'm not mad at you, helping you thru the grieving process, accepting Kelli's death, working thru your mother's death, that's my commitment to you, but that requires your commitment as well."

"I am…committed…I've been here almost everyday for weeks."

"We've made a lot of progress, there's no doubt about that, but the question is…why didn't you tell me Kelli was dead?"

"I don't know, I…figured you'd think I was crazy, you know, trying to put my marriage back together with a dead woman."

I won't tell her I'm already dead, what Lucy surely sees, these last weeks my long suicide note, a dark idea that comes and goes with the morning paper, what I never bother to read, what Maria Elena gathers up for the recycling, always wondering to herself why I still get it and shrugging and answering herself without answering. Everyday another day, the sure momentum of monotony, what we come to understand without thinking, a photo of a mountain in the Angeles Forest on fire on the front page of the Monday Times, a particular moment preserved on what we've made of a tree beneath a blue Best Buy store ad printed plastic bag, another epic disaster that won't touch us until it burns the house down. Newspapers are like that, always what's already happened and nothing of what's coming except for a guess at the weather.

"We all grieve in our own way. If we live long enough, we'll see people we love die, there's no way around that. There's no prescribed way to move through grief, we have to find what works for us, but there are things we can do together to help you move on."

"I don't expect to move on, Hannelore, I don't even deserve to."

"What makes you think you don't deserve to?"

"I don't know, I just don't. Kelli was way too good for me, I always knew that. Before her...it was just strippers and groupie chicks...and that studio exec, she was the worst of the lot."

"It's common to feel a sense of guilt when you're grieving, but go easy with yourself."

"What if the guilt is real?"

"Michael, you couldn't have done anything about Kelli's death."

"Well I'm not going to get over it...I don't even want to...I don't even know where to aim without her."

"As intense as your relationship was it's going to take time, but you'll move forward with your life."

"Maybe I've had enough, you know, like that's all the good luck I'm going to get...I've been pretty lucky so far...maybe my luck's run up."

"You have a lot of life left, Michael. You've been fortunate, yes, but you've had to overcome a lot as well. Don't discount yourself and your abilities, I don't think your life is just a matter of luck."

"So why should I be alive and Kelli be dead? It's bullshit."

"I suppose that's the challenge of mankind. We're all just trying to answer the big question why."

"Why's a tough gig."

"It's hard to see the big picture sometimes, especially when we're in the midst of things, but the most difficult periods of life are where we grow the most."

"You'd think I'd have figured things out by now...you know. Maybe I could have held onto Kelli...and maybe she wouldn't have been on the canyon road in the middle of the night and she'd be alive right now."

"It's...a real loss...but we don't control the world, we just live in it the best we can. Kelli was doing her best as were you. It's a gift to her memory that you're in therapy...and it's her gift to you that you had a place to go."

**YOUR PAST IS BEST GUESS
OF YOUR FUTURE**

PEKING NOODLE CO

Everything started the day she stopped, this life I'd live out, the old man standing in place like he'd lose his spot in line otherwise. I was eight when she died, a kid and a kind of magic, what I could find and deem lucky and stuff down into my pockets all with one spell. I hardly ever thought about her after, I never thought about her as anything but dead, like dying was the only thing she did that mattered, like the door nailed Jesus above the altar, the plaster white and blue Saint Mary sadly waiting out front of the church for a ride that never comes.

I don't remember what he said when he told me, I only remember the silence after, a nothingness filling in behind me as I ran straight out the house and across our crabgrass yard, a green we could never get rid of or keep. The old man was somehow there just as the sounds all started again, the sound of tires skidding somewhere in my head and in the heat coming off the asphalt, and voices and his voice, his hand around my arm pulling me back into the yard like I'd run thru a closed sliding glass door, him sputtering over his shoulder, his mother just died, like she was someone he didn't know. A drawn out Chevy Townsman wagon slowly starting down the street again like all the dreams we'll sleep and not remember.

The big road that ran thru town went from the lake all the way south to Florida, what was the only way before the freeway, what the old man said like he knew, but I never asked, the idea of an ocean at the other end like a heaven or a second chance. Our street only ran from one road to another and went nowhere on its own. It had wires hung from creosote poles and two wires to our chalk box house, one for electricity and one for the phone, and planted trees in front that never seemed to grow and a narrow driveway and a spare concrete walkway and two stairs to a jilted front door. It's where we lived, she lived there too, but she would die someplace else, somewhere with a saint's name two towns over. I never saw her in the hospital, what they thought was best. I would only see her again the day they buried her, painted perfect and put in a box, the old man standing next to her looking more dead than her. She was my mother, but she was my father's wife.

We would go home after, after the casket closed, before the funeral home men and two men in bluish city service coveralls lowered her into the ground. We would go home and change out of our new suit coats and pants and stiff collared button shirts, what we bought at the JC Penney the day after she died. The old man carefully hung them on their hangers and wrapped them in the clear plastic bags they came in and put them away in his closet. They're still there like an old Bible he won't chance throwing out. He thumbs thru them every anniversary or holiday or birthday along with his other old clothes, what he wore as a young man, what he wore with her, what he remembers, his memory like a row of loose teeth.

Everything around me is in boxes now, everything is between here and someplace else. Everywhere is burning or burnt down and still there's traffic and Hollywood gossip and the havoc of Westside housewives having lunch at Huckleberry. I'm in the house, what's left of me. The real estate agent wants to wait until after the fires to show it, what she says like she's waiting for the weather to clear. She wants to stage it with some interior designer she works with, someone to "make the house look beautifully lived in" instead of me and my jingle jangle. I know what she means, I've never really lived anywhere. I'm always in between things, always between here and there, between bumming rides and a beater car of my own, boxed apartments and just places to sleep, sideways glances and long stares in their eyes. This was my first house, our house, Kelli's really.

The County Sheriff began mandatory evacuations in the upper canyon last night, eight to midnight, and for our part of the mountain early this morning. There's a ring to the emptiness, a bell you don't hear, but feel, the wind raking around the few old timers that refuse to leave. The air is tight, weighed down with smoke so it seems the sun can't even rise up all the way, a midday gloaming like some beautiful strung out chick on the Strip, supernatural and broken down, long legs and skinned knees. The fire is beyond its flames, ageless trees burnt up in a matter of minutes, all those suns and rains gone on to something else now, something bigger than what's burned so that it's singed even our smallest ideas.

I'll wait now for what it seems we're all waiting for, for a long dreamless sleep, for God or good, for what we try not to think about and live our lives careening towards. I don't have the guts to do it myself, I'll let the fire cut me down and send me to smoke. I googled "burned at the stake" last night before everything went out. It seems it's best to do it big, to let the smoke do you in before the flames. I'm not afraid so much as sad and maybe relieved to finally know how it all ends. There's a comfort in any sort of certainty, so this is what Lucy sees when she looks me in the eye....

I'm on the bed with my boots on, what Kelli would have flipped out about. The thought of it makes me smile and leaves me wishing I could laugh and trying to remember her laugh. There's a kind of quiet to the Santa Anas, the air so full of sound there's no other sound, too much of anything becomes nothing. Something suddenly cracks that silence, something so loud it rattles the walls and the window glass and somewhere deep in the well of me. I look up at the ceiling beams and then out the bedroom window in time to see a super scooper plane fly over the house and dump its water just across the canyon to the back. The fire has made its way up to the top of the mountain a half mile away. What was a lullaby of smoke has become a chaos of flames and jet engines and the haze of pink fire retardant or the thunder of 1500 gallons of water at once. And everything is now and only and in an all together different wind. Wildfires this size make their own weather, everything rising up with the heat and crashing down with the weight of all the fire has dragged up into the air. The house is in it, I am in it, part of the fire's storm, its life sucking at my life, all my atoms and energy being torn away from me.

"What the fuck?...oh shit..."

The dog from down the street, a graceless mix of sorts, has come barking at the bedroom's French doors. She's frantic at the window glass, her eyes are open black, she is animal and instinct and only what can keep her alive. Kelli called her Tasha, but her name is something else. Kelli fed her table scraps, what she collected and saved in the fridge in an aluminum pie pan she'd set aside for the dog. She never came around after Kelli moved out like the dog knew something I didn't. I'd see her lying in the same spot of shade on the road as I would drive down the canyon into town each day. She wouldn't move except to pick her head up slightly, sideways, and watch me go by like I'm a two-street town Memorial Day parade oddity missing a limb.

She's seen me on the bed, it's too late to do nothing, our eyes have met, her barking becoming a desperate whine.

"Hey girl, its okay...go on home now."

I sound ridiculous, my voice thin thru the cellophane smile I've put on, my eyebrows arched with expectation as if she's going to wag her tail and go running down the street home.

"Fuck...okay...hold on."

The door bangs open the instant I turn the handle, all her being leaned against it, her big head and bigger awkward body thrust between the door jam and my leg, her nails skidding across the hard wood floor. It is a sound you feel in the back of your throat, something to make you swallow hard and squint your eyes. It is the blur of panic and the sharp detail of fear all at once. It seems to embarrass us both.

"It's okay, it's okay, easy now..."

I reach down and get a hold of her, my hands around the backsides of her jaw. I press my head to hers, my nose just above her nose, my eyes at her eyes. I can feel the life in her, her blood just beneath her fur, her breath below my chin. The moment is crystalline, a diamond hard pattern come together. This dog is a life, and I am a life, some magic beyond our grasp or God and as simple as a field mouse. We are the same or not even the same, but one thing. And everything is sped up, everything has gone quiet and slowed down and focused to a point.

"It's okay...it's okay, I'll get us out of here."

My voice is sure and I am somehow sure, like the old days when I was young and full of blood, steel-toed and standing straight up, running where I could have walked to and only saying what needed to be said.

"All right...where the fuck is my Carhart?"

Maria Elena has packed everything in boxes, boxes stacked up two and three high so I can only see what's written on the top box. I start taking them down and throwing them to the side, boxes with "guest bedroom" or "living room" written out with a black Sharpie and filled with things that have no everyday purpose, things that can only be explained by a place, things that have a time and a memory and eight boxes of "winter clothes," a California winter, what is its own kind of cold, a coastal air that gets in thru the cracks. The dog looks on like I know what I'm doing, some strange trust that's been bred into her kind, the poor thing. I take a winter clothes box and tear the tape across the top that's holding it closed. It's filled with Kelli's sweaters, her baby blue cashmere sweater on top. And for a moment there is nothing else, but her.

"Kell…"

Her name breathes out of me like it left an empty space where it was, like I only have so many times to say her name and I've almost run out. I grab her sweater like I have to, I have to, and bring it to my face. And for a moment I could be anywhere and anytime, on the Coast Highway with her in my hands and the wind off the ocean against my back, her hair on my face…. All these moments twisting down my spine and along some Einstein line into space, out where I can never touch them, but see them when the day turns to night. And it comes to me just then that I'm not angry anymore, that I never was, that I've been broken-hearted all this time, but all I ever knew was how to fight. I can feel the ache in the hollow parts of me, past the muscle and tendon, bone, fascia and gut, what always left me swinging before, knuckle busted and spitting blood. I take the punch straight on and turn around, fat lipped and knocked out of air.

"Kelli...I'm sorry..."

The sound of an explosion pulls me out of my head and back into the wind and the smoke. The propane tank of the old red cabin house across the canyon has ruptured sending a thirty foot plume of fire into the black sky.

"Fuck."

I tear at another box, then another and finally amongst a rain jacket and pants is my Carhart jacket, union made back in the day, a masterpiece of American when it mattered, jobs that were sent off overseas, to China or Bangladesh so they've never been the same. My Carhart is faded and just the right kind of fucked up, canvas duck cloth worn at the cuffs and at the elbows and at the corduroy collar and stiff still like an old man with a sharp memory who still works everyday. I throw it on over my t-shirt and grab my old raiders cap, Ray Ban Aviators, button Levis and my old lace up boots.

"That's as fireproof as you're going to get, Mikey."

I can feel the blood rush tight to my arms like the old days, like I'm ready to fight, a Mike before I was Michael.... I bite down hard on my jaw and screw down my stare, my eyes just below the brim of my cap. I am a line, a straight line from here to there. I grab my old Leatherman for luck and push it down into my front pocket, Kelli's cashmere sweater still in my hand...

"Come on, Tasha, let's go."

**AN OLD FRIEND WILL MAKE
YOU FEEL YOUNG AGAIN**

PEKING NOODLE CO

Bad luck turns to good luck and good luck to the mundane, everything becomes something else. Every wish come true turns to everyday scrabble, while the mishap and missed chances come to be all we remember and love. Every path runs in two directions. All the rivers run one way. Time is science and make believe, days are long and life is short.

Everything is breaking down, everywhere is burning, turning to ash, to carbonates and oxides, becoming black. There is no stopping this fire, what they're calling the Trippet Ranch Fire, forty years of brush built up and weeks of high winds. They name them now, the biggest fires, to grasp what they can't contain, but this fire is bigger than its flames, bigger than what it's left pitch behind it. It has reached into our hearts, into our dreams, up to our petty secret ambitions. It is bigger than God. It is here and now and God is only someday at best.

The long fish is in its tank, in every tick of time and between. It is temporary and enough. It is everything ever, it is nothing and nothingness and some part of all of this, of all of us, of a universe cut from chaos and a precise kind of luck. It is eyed and eyed, always watching, never looking, swimming side to side, swimming faster and faster until it breaks up and into the air, onto the table for two, into the lap of the Westside woman sitting there, and finally to the floor below. Lucy looks up, but not to the table, but to where the long fish's eye is dreaming, to someplace west and to something only the two of them will see.

"Oh my God...oh...help!"

"Tony, qu na long li yu...Bobby, xian zai ca zhuo zi qu..."

The two at the table have stood up and stepped back. They are standing in the middle of the restaurant like they've waded into cold water, the woman screaming so even the people that speak English don't know what she's saying, the man wide-eyed and open-mouthed and perfectly silent, is easily understood. Tony is at the table as if he was never anywhere else, handing the woman a white linen napkin and respectfully nodding to the man as he bows down and picks up the long fish with his hands as sure as two old books, his every move connected to the next as if it were all a part of a well rehearsed play, a story we've been read a thousand times as children before it's been packed up and put away. Bobby arrives like a one man band, squatting down to pick up the broken plates and glass and spilt food and tipped bowls. Everything done with angled arms and turned out feet, everywhere knees and elbows and this here and that goes, everything back on the table and taken up in the tablecloth at it's corners and dumped into the bus cart crash with one throw, as Tony slips into the kitchen with the long fish unnoticed, the perfect magic trick.

"Tony, put fish here."

Lucy is in the kitchen alone, the kitchen crew know enough to go out to the alley and wait. She is filling a large stock pot from the faucet in the sink. Tony has backed his way into and stopped just on the other side of the swinging door in, the long fish in his hands, his blue veined arms extended out away from his body like a pale Christ posed for a painting. He looks Lucy straight in the eyes, Lucy stares back like they're playing Russian roulette with a fully loaded gun. Nothing is said. It is the sort of silence that fills the room, any sound pushed to the walls, down to the floor and out under the doors. Tony places the fish in the pot like he might lay an old relative to rest, his eyes still on Lucy's eyes. Lucy lives out his death until it's done and turns away to the stock pot in the sink, speaking with her slight shoulder to Tony, she's seen enough.

"Take pot to car."
"Why you speak English to Tony?"
"We only one in kitchen speak English, they not know, not need whisper, people alway hear whisper."
"Where you go?"
"Where I alway going."

Tony breathes out without sighing, bending slightly forward and then back, breathing in, pulling everything around his spine and out again. His brow is creased with time, with suns and fluorescent work lights. He is a man. He is a thousand generations at once. He holds down the earth, he holds up the sky. He never lets on. He is a grain of rice. He will carry the stock pot and the long fish to the old car Lucy drives now, what her father drove before her, a 1972 two door pastel lime Lincoln Continental Mark IV with hideaway headlights, a white vinyl roof and opera windows. It was Chen Liu's only car, what he bought new with cash and a keen eye like he was picking a fish from the tank. The fat white salesman sneered when Liu said "pastel lime" and asked if he didn't mean yellow and blinked his eyes like a silent movie star when Liu stacked the cash for the car on his desk, nine thousand, six hundred and forty three dollars. "No yellow, pastel lime, thank you."

"Mei geren dou huiqu gongzuo."

Tony speaks Chinese with short breaths, he saves his air for when he's quiet.

"Hao hao gong zuo. "

The cooks and prep cooks, dishwashers and a busboy shuffle back in the door and disappear behind their chores. The engine starts with the first turn of the key and a slight press on the pedal like Chen Liu taught her. Lucy and the long fish float away, the pastel lime Continental mixing in the shadows of the buildings and the slim interruptions of light between them, the tires hiss on the wet blacktop, there's always water in the alley somehow. Tony watches the car until it disappears around the corner to the right, to Hill Street and then Chinatown. He closes his eyes and listens for the Continental's certain engine, something separate from all the other sounds, second hand sounds and echoes, all of it only after it's happened, a ghost world between a silence and the hum and the hullabaloo. He opens his eyes again and heads back into the kitchen, the rusted steel grate door closes behind him like the end of a sentence, every sentence a little life and death.

Lucy looks just over the wheel, thru the long curve of the windshield, thru the light of a worn red sun and a typecast sky. It is a light that can only happen here, something queer and familiar still, something ephemeral and forever on film. It is stretched out like a Technicolor movie made to fit a t.v., Instamatic, Kodachrome, Polaroid and Fuji. It is palm trees on the Strip and the bright billboard hopes behind it all. All the promises of this big west spelled out in nine letters in the hills and sworn to and broken in the same breath. Los Angeles is all that or nothing. Lucy pulls down the sun visor and pushes the gas pedal to the floor.

The Continental's radio is a tuning dial and a volume knob, five station preset push buttons and an am/fm stereo switch. It is mechanical, physical, on and off. It is obvious and still in between, where everything today is a digital absolute and almost only a ghost of what once had a hand. It is set in order to Chen Liu's stations still, am radio news and the Dodgers, fm public radio and gumball oldies. A radio voice tells her that Topanga, Tuna, Big Rock and Los Flores Canyons are closed, that the PCH is closed between Sunset and Kanan Dume Road. An L.A. County Fire Department spokesperson reads a prepared statement, what sounds below Lucy's thoughts like traffic noise, like anything you hear, but don't listen to and only notice once it stops...

"Cal Fire has 300 firefighters, two fixed wing aircraft and four water dropping helicopters currently deployed to the Santa Monica mountains Trippet Ranch Fire..."

A man driving a white Chevy van glances Lucy's way as she passes. She sees beyond him to an April 22nd, to the man in a yellowing white t-shirt and underwear clutching his chest in the mirror in a small thirties era yellow and turquoise tiled bathroom. Lucy feels the cool floor on the side of her face as she and the long fish speed by.

"The fire as reported by county fire officials crossed the break at Topanga State Park at 8pm last night and is moving west and south into the Fernwood and Big Rock neighborhoods. Both these areas underwent mandatory evacuations facilitated by the Los Angeles County Sheriff's Department yesterday and remain closed. Cal Fire has confirmed that over one hundred structures have been damaged or destroyed in the Topanga post office tract. we cannot overstate the danger and unpredictability of this fire..."

The long fish looks up at Lucy with cataract eyes, but seeing is for those that look. All of us now are little Gods with lightning in our hands, always staring at our phones, at omnipotent Google searches and live streaming Facebook feeds. And still it seems we can't do a thing. Knowing is the end of us. Everything wrong was right once, it's better to wonder than to know.

"The national weather service has forecast continuing weather conditions that have been fueling the Trippet Ranch Fire and the active wildfires in Los Angeles county. Record high temperatures, winds of 30 to 60 miles per hour and desert humidity levels are to be expected for the next three days. These conditions have facilitated an unprecedented number of fires in the county and across the state..."

A chance eye from a Hispanic man in a faded Camry, an overcast November 9th, a punk kid driving too fast in a bent Ford F-150 pickup, next September 2nd, his 22nd birthday, a gun shot thru the roof of his mouth, Lucy's lip twitches, she doesn't notice, the long fish stops and starts its circle again the other way.

"We want to thank the 6000 Cal Fire firefighters and the 2000 firefighters from as far as Arizona, New Mexico, Colorado, Oregon and Canada, and local and county law enforcement for their tireless efforts. As of thirteen hundred hours, 1 pm, the Trippet Ranch Fire is zero percent contained. I can take your questions now...."

Lucy has pushed these wheels past any prayer or promise, and still the Continental heaves itself down the freeway like an aging star, like anything that never slows down, but burns until it stops. A tack of spent oil fills the car and everywhere down the road behind it, the engine at its end, a V-8, 3 speed Detroit motor dream, culled and cast and finally past by. The speedometer needle leans over like a long tree threatening to fall, 90, 95, 100, 105. Lucy keeps both hands on the wheel, her eyes straight ahead out the windshield and straight behind in the rear view mirror, but she knows neither of them matter, all that matters is here. All that matters is now.

The 10 runs west from Florida to Santa Monica and the McClure Tunnel where it becomes the California 1 out the other side. All that way across a big-boned America and it never sees the ocean, like a long kiss and nothing else, but luck can be like that, a beginning and an end all at once. The fire smoke is black above the mountains, then white like it's something else as it stretches out across the ocean sky. Lucy lets down the Lincoln's windows, the air is a shock of heat, even at the beach, and soot. The Ferris wheel on the pier turns round and round like the careless cotton candied kids spinning on the boardwalk, the boardwalk teaming with t-shirt tourist gawking at the smoke. The Continental burns down the highway, the long fish swims in a circle in its pot.

Lucy will pull the husk of the Lincoln into the grocery store parking lot just before the traffic light at sunset and the Sheriff's road block. She will wait with the motor running, her blood pushing red through her arteries and back blue through her veins, the long fish breathing water, the fire burning brush and combustible matter and oxygen in the air. What will happen next is not of words. Lucy knows there are things that cannot be said, they are too small to see how and too big to know why.

A Chinese woman in a red silk dress with a two foot long dragon fish in a 20 quart stock pot, in a 1972 pastel lime Lincoln Continental, will drive through the Chevron gas station, behind and beyond the established road block and continue north on the PCH while two County Sheriffs and two California Highway Patrolmen stand by on the road, leaning against their cars, talking like cops, breathing like fat predators after coming upon a kill, one turning cars away with a distracted and still remotely exasperated sweep of his hand, their everyday minds ticking with everyday thoughts like their digital wrist watches silently dividing out the time. But time is like that, everyone with their own time, fast or slow, and everyone with the same time still somehow, and nothing we can keep or hold. It's hard to know when it's time. It's hard to know what you've seen and what you haven't seen. Science seems the opposite of magic, yet science tells us that matter is mostly empty space. I suppose it's a matter of luck to see anything at all.

**SEEING IS BELIEVING AND
BELIEVING IS BLIND**

PEKING NOODLE CO

You can find your way without knowing where you're going, something found was something lost. Every big bang had the providence of luck, in the beginning even God had his fingers crossed. It's hard to know what to do, where to go, how to get there. We wander and wonder still like we never left the house, like the road was just something else to ponder. I always figured it was best to keep moving, that the answers would come along the way. I've gone as far as I can go now, the far side of the fault line and the ocean's edge. I've gone as far as I can go and still it seems I don't know a damn thing. If this is the end, I've come a long way, but it's never the years, so much, as the mileage.

The old man never bought a used car past his first car when he was in high school. He'd always tell me, "You're just buying someone else's problem." I suppose he was right, but I never listened. I turn the truck's door lock with the key, the mechanism rolls over like an old hand, arthritic, but sure, snapping a thumb and a middle finger. It's what I have left, a 1970 Chevy C-10 short box pickup. It steers like shit, but it starts easy and stops hard since I had Jorge fit it with disc brakes, and these days, what's left is what matters.

"Come on girl, get in...come on now, it's ok...come on...all right, good girl."

Tasha scrambles up onto the driver side floor and across to the other side. I turn back and look at the house, the sky battered black and blue behind it. It looks smaller than when we bought it, like it wore away with the two of us, a painted wood box, a stone rock and mortar chimney to keep it in place. It was built in 1928 and added onto every generation until it had more doors than rooms. It was the first place I've ever owned and a home I suppose.

I get in the truck, the springs push up through the old seat like they do, reminding me that we're both wearing thin. I wait to close the door. When I close the door and drive away it's done. Everything that was us, our beginnings and our ends, the atoms of her that are left, will be gone, turned to carbon black and burnt away to something else. I wonder what I can remember of it, the house the way it is, the mountain and the trees. It's the trees I'll miss. I close down hard on my eyes and press it all into some part of me, some old part of my brain I don't use that has room. I wonder what I remember of Kelli and what I've just made up to keep my story straight. I wonder what anyone can remember of a life like this, my life stretched out like a long road I can't see end to end, and the lines worn away and hardly a road sign so I never really know where I am, only that I'm moving on.

I put the key in the ignition without thinking and turn it, a slight push on the pedal, the 350 sparks and rumbles, she's always been a quick start. I put it in drive like so many times before, but this time it seems to have purpose, like everything I do from here on will mean something. We make our way down the road towards the canyon road, the fire coming up the hillside from the valley. The air is everywhere and riddled with smoke. The trees are filled with wind, with woe, bent over or broken in half, branch bustles and leaves left scattered across the road, a power line swinging down, but there's no power. Nothing is still, even the houses look to be shaking in the wind. Everyone has evacuated out, there's not a car anywhere, except for an old sunburnt Volvo that hasn't moved in years, grass grown up around its wheels and over the rusted bumpers. I have the windows up, the radio off, the a/c on, but it's not enough for the heat. The wind is so loud it's quiet. The houses on the valley side of the road have given in and are just a part of the fire now, Tasha is up on the bench seat barking at the flames.

"It's all right girl."

She barks right at my face in response.

"Yeah, you're right, we're probably fucked."

She turns her eyes away from me and back to the fire, barking at it like she might at the mailman. As we come around a tight turn I slam on the brakes, but it's too late, the truck's front plows into a dead Monterey pine, what folks planted here in the twenties for a start, what only made it to the drought, but not thru it, what has been dead and finally fallen across the road.

"Shit!"

I throw the truck in reverse and then park. I start to open the door as Tasha leaps across my lap, out of the truck, over the tree and down the road and out of sight.

"God damn it! Tasha, come here! Come on... fuck...really? You...fucking...bitch!"

I lock out the front wheels and jump back in the cab and close the door. I take a breath trying to get some clean air, but there's nothing that's not smoke. I can feel my arms get tight, my grip on the wheel close in, my knuckles push up, L.U.C.K. blurred across them.

"If I can pop the front bumper over the trunk the wheels should grab and we can get over this fucking thing."

I'm talking to myself, to the truck, maybe, or to God even, if he's listening. I used to say my prayers every night when I was a kid, before she died. I could never quite remember the Lord's Prayer or the Hail Marys. My prayers were sort of just Christmas list wishes and bargains back if any of it came true. I don't think any of it did, she died anyway and I never got that metal fleck red Schwinn banana bike I begged the old man for.

"All right fucker..."

The Chevy C-10 was one of the heaviest half ton pickups ever produced, the curb weight near 4000 pounds. Being a bouncer and a heavy hand you come to understand the fundamentals of physics, of mass and acceleration, that energy is neither created nor destroyed. The truck will hit the tree at 22 miles per hour, it will feel like sixty. It will push the bumper in and the tree trunk almost 4 feet forward, The front wheels will not go over the trunk, an angle that was not derived. There is no bullshitting math.

"Fuck."

I try again, this time slowly bringing the truck's bumper up over the remaining dead branches and onto the tree trunk, then stepping on it to see if I can get the truck's front wheels up on and over it, the four wheels blubbering and jumping sideways.

"Fuck!"

There is no other way, the other way is surely full of the fire behind me now. I won't make it on foot. I was going to wait it out in the house, I suppose I'll wait it out in the truck instead. I guess Tasha knew best. I feel bad for the old man, he'll have out lived her and me both.

The night she died, I laid in bed and listened into the dark, past my bedroom ceiling, above the roof and over the trees, into the street-lit sky for anything of her, for her ghost or her echo. I tried to remember her hands in my hair, shampoo in my eyes, her smell, a kiss goodnight, her voice when I wasn't in trouble. I could remember the things she said, but not the sound of what she said, like nothing had ever been hers, but taken on tick. Even her obituary in the Plain Dealer seemed like something not hers, black type on colorless pulp, what the old man cut out and glued to a piece of cardboard like stats on a Ray Fosse baseball card, a picture of the Virgin Mary on the other side instead.

"What the fuck?"

Just above the last curve in the road I see Tasha running back towards the truck, and behind her what looks to be an old Continental with no one driving. I open the truck door as if I need to be outside to make sense of it. The fire's ferment pushes inside the truck, turning everything into an Aspirin bottle cotton stopper. Tasha is barking, her mouth moving like she's barking, I don't really hear her. An old seventies Lincoln Continental floats up to the tree and comes to a long stop. I can't move or I won't. I'm just watching like I'm not a part of all this, an observer with the sound turned off or an in between station static turned up all the way on.

"Michael, we need come with you."

Lucy has appeared from around the Continental's door carrying an enormous pot. It still hasn't occurred to me that she was driving. Tasha is next to me, frantically barking at me, then at the flames, then at Lucy and the pot and finally back at me.

"Lucy?"
"Michael, fire on road behind us, we need go other way."
"Lucy...what are you doing here?"
"Come get you."

My mind has stopped, everything before me is more than it can hold. Times like this you can only think with your body, with your muscle tendon, nerve and bone. Lucy is in a red silk dress, a shock of blue eye shadow caked on above her eyes like she does, a big fish like the fish from the center tank in the restaurant in a bigger pot in Lucy's little outstretched arms. Lucy looks small without the Lucky around her, like its a part of her and now she's out here just in her shoes.

"Who's Continental is that?"
"Father car, he dead, I drive now."
"I didn't know you drive, Lucy."
"Michael, we need go, fire right behind."
"Seventy-one?"
"Michael, we need go now, all of us."
"When did they do the fold down lights? Maybe not 'til seventy-two...Lucy, is that the fish from the Lucky?"
"Yes, will be cooked fish if we not go."

Lucy walks past me with the bulk of the stock pot and the long fish inside, to the passenger side door of the truck, Tasha following behind her, but looking back at me with a mix of guilt and guile.

"Michael! Door locked..."
"Oh..yeah, sorry Lucy."

I grab the key from the ignition and open her door like we're on a first date, reaching to help her with the pot, she heaves it onto the middle of the bench seat without ceremony herself, sits next to it and lifts her legs to let Tasha climb in below and slams the door closed.

"Lucy...what about your father's car?"
"What about what?"

"We can't just leave it there."

"Michael, time to think and time to not think, only do. You need do now."

"Ok…I'm gonna move the car off the road."

The old man never drove anything nicer than a Ford LTD. He always said his first new car was his favorite, a black Mercury Comet Cyclone, a car I can only squint to remember, his '75 electric blue Chrysler Cordoba a close second. All of them were second tier cars, what you buy when you aspire to a Cadillac, to a New Yorker or a Lincoln, an end you'll likely never afford. I move the Continental's seat back and swing my legs in and close the door. I can see Lucy yelling through the truck's and the Continental's windshields, but I can't hear her with the doors closed and the wind and the fire. I sit back and let the big front seat take my weight as I take in the car. There's an epic ambit about it, a chest out proud steering wheel and the sweep of the prairie long dash, the sheer breadth of it all, something solely American and a seventies era last gasp of hope.

"Maybe the old man will buy himself something with the insurance money…something really nice."

He won't. I'm not sure he'll have anything of me other than what he already has, an old baseball mitt and my toys put away in the basement, G.I. Joe and Hot Wheels and a weary basketball hoop standing in the driveway still like some pitted monument to my misspent youth, the concrete cracked with winters and summers and tree roots from next door.

"I should have bought him a car when I was at Sony…an 8 Series or something…something…nice…"

I'm whispering, staring down at the wheel, at my hands around it like I could somehow hold on, a fading L.U.C.K. tattooed on my knuckles, a stab at chance from a different time and a seemingly different hand. The old man would say, if wishes were horses, the Irish would ride all day…. I never really got what he meant then, but his somedays were all pretty much yesterdays.

   "Michael!"

Lucy's face is at the driver side window of the car. Her eye shadow an impossible azure by the broken light of the sun and the fire on the other side of the road.

   "Jesus Lucy, you scared the shit out of me."
   "You scare me, think you dead in car, too much smoke. What you do? We need go now."
   "Yeah…ok…um…let's go."
   "Michael, fire on road behind car."
   "It's probably burning the other way too, Lucy. When I left the house the fire was coming up the back. It wasn't going to take long before it got to the house…and everything else."
   "Can't stay here, here no good."
   "Yeah…"

I don't know what to say, sometimes you can only do. We run back and slide into the truck, onto the bench seat, the long fish in its pot between us, Tasha on the floor beneath Lucy's dangling feet. I turn the truck around with a wrench resolve, reverse then drive, and drive a line up the road into the fire, a strict chaos of rote chemical reactions, molecular bonds breaking apart, new patterns taking hold, propane tanks exploding somewhere, eucalyptus trees burning up in one breath. The old oaks hold on, they've been here before, the original Topanga houses, what were just shotgun shacks in the twenties, what are seven figure charmers now, finally giving in to the flames. I look right at Lucy, but she's looking away, her eyes straight up the road and to the fire to the right, the long fish languid in its stock pot.

And for a moment, what seemed longer, a lifetime or all of time, maybe, Lucy turns and looks me right in the eye, and I look at her. She is an old woman, her hair white as white, she has on no makeup, but for the reddest lipstick wrote out from a shaky hand. We do not speak and there is no sound, everything is stopped, then there are words, probably thoughts, what I can hear and not hear, my voice in my head...

"Are we dead?"
"No."
"Where are we?"
"Hard to know, you see what Lucy see when Lucy look."
"Am I going to see my death?"
"No."
"Why are you old?"
"You see Lucy death, but you afraid, not really see."
"I don't understand."
"You will."

The roar of the wind and the fire and the torque of the truck fill back into my head again like a rogue wave ruining a seaside picnic as Lucy turns her eyes away and looks up the road.

"Need get to water tank."

"What do you mean?"

"Need get to water tank, fire man be there, they not let water tank burn. Fire man keep way to tank good."

"There's one at the top of the mountain...yeah, that makes sense...ok...hang on, we got some gnarly shit to get through."

My mind is struck with the white haired Lucy, with what I saw and wouldn't see. We won't speak again until we get to the two large County Water Department water tanks a mile up the road. Lucy was right, the road there was still open, the fire kept down with water dropping helicopters and a pumper towards the top. We pull up to a red Chevy Suburban, Commander painted along the rear quarter panel.

"You folks should have evacuated last night!"

"Yeah, I know...sorry."

I'm yelling through the rolled down window to be heard, so loud that it seems like I'm not sorry. I'm not sorry, but I don't want him to know.

"I got no hands to take you down now, you're going to have to wait it out until I can get a shift change. Put your truck over to the left of the tanks, get it tight to the fence, I got to keep room for crew."

"Ok."

I feel like a scolded school kid put out in the hall, class continuing on the other side of the closed door. I roll up the window as I steer the truck along the fence.

"Michael, we not wait."

"What? Lucy you wanted to get to the water tanks, we're at the water tanks."

"Here no good."

"What do you mean no good?"

"He not make it."

"What you mean? He won't make it, like he's going to die? Now?"

"Yes, he die today."

"Lucy, what the fuck! We need to tell him."

"We not change thing, even if want to. Lucy see what Lucy see."

"But Lucy..."

"You think Lucy not try before?"

"Yeah, but we just...we can't just leave him here to die."

"Then you see him die too."

"Lucy?"

"Lucy try save people, it not matter, die just like Lucy see, Lucy just there instead of not there."

"But..."

"No change thing, life and death have own time, we not change."

"I don't know...fuck! How do you do it? Fuck...I...I can't handle this. I.."

"Michael, everything die."

"Yeah, I know that Lucy, but knowing when, and not trying to save him, I don't know how to live with that. I don't know how you've done it all these years."

"Lucy not control, Lucy try many time and fail. You not save Kellee, not matter what you do. You heart saw death all round her, I know you love very much, do anything, Lucy do anything, but there no changing Kellee time. Need accept."

I look across the blacktop to the commander, to the crew at the pumper, a helicopter above us we can only hear.

"Are they all going to die today?"

"Lucy not know, not see. Fire come fast, no way escape."

"I'm sorry, Lucy."

"You ok, not need be sorry."

"No...I've always treated you like it was some sort of cool party trick or something, but it's not...it's...it's a fucking curse."

"We need go now, Michael, this place bad place to be."

"We're going to have to drive through the fire to get out of here."

"Yes, drive through fire."

I shift in my seat, set my weight right like I'm ready for a fight, my left hand on the wheel, my right on the gear shift. I look Lucy straight in the eyes again, the old, white haired Lucy looking back at me.

"Lucy, is this how..."

"This not how you die, Michael. You not die today."

"Yeah...ok. I'm sorry, Lucy...I'll never ask again."

I put the truck in drive, push my jaw out and my foot down, the gas pedal to the floor. The carburetor quaffs a mix of air and a flood of 89 octane, the engine's eight cylinders spark, the truck's rebuilt 350 opens its eyes. We're pressed back into the bench seat as the truck lurches forward, the truck tails to the left just missing the chain link fence as we tear across the blacktop surrounding the water tanks. I can see the commander's head turn around like a wary herd animal, he's probably yelling, I'm afraid to look and look into his eyes, my eyes straight ahead, on the road and into the fire.

**STEEL STRONGEST THAT
BEEN THROUGH THE FLAME**
PEKING NOODLE CO

Everything changes. Everything will forever be the same. There is nothing new in this world or in the next, nothing that hasn't always been since the big bang or God's first big breath out. Whatever you believe in, it ends all the same. It seems everything is broke apart by time and bound together again with science or a lashing of luck and a kind of hand magic. We are, all of us, of the past, all of us pieces of something else. We are dust and dust, ashes and ashes, and something of love, something that can't be made, made bigger or broke down, thought up or forgotten.

It's hard to remember. And despite everything we do to forget, strung out sweat lodges and week-long silent yoga retreats, tantric rock star ayahuasca acid trips or just everyday Pico Boulevard cheap bottle drinking bar benders, we won't forget. We can't. Our memories are set in our bones and in the grind of our joints, what add up to a life and maybe some sort of knowing, but I'm not sure we'll ever know what it all meant. It's hard to know anything at all. We'll never know everything that burned, what was here and what has gone and gone on to nothing. But nothing is a big idea and likely the start of everything we think of as something.

The mountain is burning or burnt down, houses to stone foundations, rock chimneys hanging on, the skeleton of a stove or a dishwasher, hollowed out cars, the remaining frames left like an old idea you had and never mustered, the memories of trees wrote out in rings in their wood, a warp and weft of suns and seasons, winter rains when it rained, what were caught by roots and not run on to the ocean, water pulled up by a moon full of wanting, all of it only smoke now across the sky, and ash that will mix in the ground and grow an oak again, a sage brush or a hold of chaparral.

The little man can only hold what he didn't have, give away what he lost, speak out under his breath and tack to a Facebook page. He talks to the t.v., to the radio, to the flat grained faces on his whittled down desktop computer screen. He walks in on his shoes, picks at his nails, rubs his small hands together under a Bible book light. He only knows the day by where he is, the time by the traffic, the year by the years since mother died. He only sees what isn't there, between what is there and what is gone now. He only hears what they said, the words ringing in his head, in his head like the last gallon of gas in a five gallon can.

The little man slouches forward, turns a worn key amongst a scatter of keys hung on a plain ring and a yellow plastic tab that said something once about a family name insurance agency in the Valley, his round chin over his two scant hands on the wheel, a 1998 Ford Ranger

4 cylinder blunders and sputters, a radio am starts, a clutter of a/c and a fan turned to its maximum, a five speed manual, all of it on and on all the way and not enough still to make any difference, a hand crank window, a plastic center console cup holder filled with dull nickels and grimy pennies and somehow always shiny dimes and never a quarter when he needs one. He lets off the clutch, his Dollar Store foot on the pedal for gas, the truck's tires worn to the radials absently roll over the fresh swept sidewalk into the filthy oil soaked street. Everything is small around him and he is small, but for the fire he lit, what has grown bigger than his dreams, his sticks and stone dreams, his pushed down, picked on, pat little dreams. By luck his smut match strike will be the third largest fire in California history when it's over, but even the brightest sun is just a star in another sky. Luck is like that, what it gives it takes, what was you and your doing becomes luck and luck's instead.

The little man drives across the Valley, Victory to Ventura, to Sepulveda, to Santa Monica Boulevard to the beach, everything always surface streets, old diners and old shop owner shops. Every road becomes one road finally. Everything always goes west.

"Michael, where you house?"

"We passed it, Luce. I mean...we passed where it was... It looked like it was pretty much gone."

"Only thing, material thing not matter, life matter."

"Yeah, I know."

"Hour go you ready give up life, you not care you live or die, then life remind you life matter, you not care about thing anymore. You remember you heart, heart tell you what matter."

"The house...was, you know, all I had left of Kelli and me. I know it's crazy, but it's probably why I kept putting off selling it...I couldn't let her go."

"Kellee not gone, nothing gone, everything become something else."

"Yeah, but we sort of...I don't know how to say it...rub off on stuff, does that make sense? You know, like her things were...were part of her."

"Part you now, you memory, you hold in heart, you heart what matter, life what matter, now matter, past thing not matter."

We will sit quiet as we make our way down the road. It is like night the smoke is so thick, the only light that of a broke down sun somewhere and the flames. Most of the old market on the canyon road has burned, what's left is still burning, what County Fire 69 had to give up, but there's room enough in the parking lot to turn and turn the truck around.

"Michael, what you do?"
"You're right, Lucy, life is what matters..."
"Here no good, Michael, we need go to ocean."
"We're going back to get those other firemen."
"Lucy not know if we can save, not see in eye."
"We can try...I'm not dying today...and neither are you. There's no use us wasting our day's worth of immortality."

Lucy looks straight in my eyes like she wants to be sure, then away. The silence fills in around our last words, what become just thoughts, the white haired Lucy next to me when I look, it seems the silence is enough said. Tasha presses her head between Lucy's dangling feet, the long fish swims a small circle in its pot. I watch the road, the Chevy's hood out in front of us like a kind of old faith, my mountain town burning down around me. And in just one breath out I am empty, the life I've been carrying all this time behind me and burned away, and all that's left of me are the parts that matter, fast twitch muscle fiber, tested tendon, ligament and marrow bone, a narrow nerve for the road, an instinct for life and now. Everything is now, everything else fuel for the fire.

Wildfires at their fronts can be a hundred feet high and higher and reach 2,000 degrees and burn at ten miles per hour or faster and faster up hill. The Trippet Ranch Fire will cross Fernwood Road behind them, Dack will see it first, a fourteen year veteran, then Rivera, then Bergstrom, then Delogrice. Their only safe spot is up from the fire and up from the fire is never safe. They'll group together in the center of the road readying to deploy their fire shelters when we'll see them, when they'll see us. I'll pull the truck into the nearest driveway and back out the other way. The moment we come to a stop we feel the four of them jumping into the back, Dack last making sure the other three are in.

"Lucy, are they going to make it?"
"Not know, not see eye before they cover in foil."
"Fuck."

"No be mad, you do right thing, alway best to take chance, better than no chance."

"I think that's a fortune cookie fortune."

"Everything fortune cookie fortune."

HOPE FOR TOMORROW
LIVE FOR TODAY
PEKING NOODLE CO

Luck is the start of things, and the end of things, good or bad, like a Jesus or a small town Judas. It isn't prayed for, it isn't given or granted, luck is found, stumbled upon and dropped on our heads. Luck is lost, run up and run out when we didn't even know we'd spent it. The best of us doesn't always win, nor the worst forever lose. Luck is luck, and either way, luck is of the undeserving.

I have a story, we all have a story, a line that gets us from there to here, what we tell ourselves to get across the day, voices in our heads, looks from the neighbors as you drive by, stares that say more about them than you and still could take a tall tree down. This story is like every Bible story, come down the mountain and through the fire, a good lie and a hard truth all in one breath. I'll tell my story, but I won't believe it, I save that kind of faith for the pious and the profane alike. It is the truth, if only my truth, and something when it seems I have nothing else.

"Michael, come in, come in, my God, I don't even know what to say..."
"Hey Hannelore, thanks for seeing me."

"I'm so glad you came back, when you told me Kelli had died…well, I wasn't sure I'd see you again… And now this…it's all over the news, you're a hero!"

"I don't know about that, I…just got lucky."

"That was no matter of luck, Michael. You saved a woman's life and a group of firemen…and a dog and a…a fish I think."

"Yeah, it was a real Noah's Arc."

"Seriously, this was a very selfless act."

"I was just in the right place at the right time…or maybe the wrong place and the wrong time..?"

"Is it uncomfortable for you to accept praise?"

"I just don't think I did anything that…special or anything."

"Michael, you risked your life to save, what?, five people's lives and two animals."

"I was playing with house money."

"What do you mean by that?"

"I knew I couldn't lose."

"You had everything to lose."

"Not really."

"And why's that?"

"I mean, to be honest with you, Hannelore, I was going to wait it out in the house until the fire came…"

"You were contemplating suicide?"

"I don't know if I'd call it that."

"Let's not wrestle with semantics, Michael, letting the fire kill you is the same as you killing yourself."

"I guess, but…I don't know…. It's different now."

"How so?"

"The fire, it…changed things."

"What changed?"

"I don't know…me, I guess…life…everything. I saw things, things most people aren't ever going to see. I…can't really explain it…"

"You literally walked through fire, Michael, I don't see how that wouldn't change you. You told me once that 'why' isn't for us to know, so perhaps you could tell me 'what' happened and maybe we can process that together."

"I'm not sure I even know what happened."

"Do your best."

"It's pretty weird."

"I've been a couples counselor for thirty years, my idea of weird is likely something most people could never imagine…"

"Yeah, straight ass people can be into some crazy shit….

"So what happened?"

"It kind of all started with the dog…the trees, me, everything…like we're all connected. I couldn't let that dog die and I guess that meant I wasn't dying either."

It's hard to tell a story when you're in it, when you don't know the beginning or the end and the middle is clouded with smoke. It's hard to know how small we are or how to hold all the pieces of a big world poured into our penny hands. It seems we're left to believing in what we can, in it all adding up to something, even if it is too big to ever count. What the simplest of animals seem to know better than me, and that all this is one thing, everything tied together with gut string and cartilage and a shared breath breathed into us all until even God makes sense, what seems to science as math, what looks like luck to me. This place will do that to you, and fire changes the view. Sometimes it's what's not there that matters most.

"It's a very Buddhist train of thought, Michael."

"Well I'm not giving up meat.... I guess I'm not that enlightened."

"Noted. So that explains the dog, but the woman...and the firemen...and how do you come about rescuing a fish?"

"I've told you about my friend, Lucy that owns the Chinese place I've been going to since I first started bouncing on the Strip."

"Yes, I remember you speaking of her."

"Lucy...knows things...and I think the fish knows things too...the fish is from the restaurant...I told you it was going to get weird...anyway, Lucy knew I needed help."

"That's quite a friend you have that would put themselves in harm's way for you, though it sounds like she's the one that wound up needing saving, her and her fish."

"Yeah, she got herself in some serious shit for me, that's for sure...but like I said, Lucy knows things. I think she knew the only way to save me...was for me to save her."

Lucy is of the earth and air, water and fire, her birth year a fire year, what she was told, and that the day was a warm day and raining. Lucy stands on the ground, looks straight ahead, sees what is shown her, hears what is said. There are a thousand years between each beat of her heart, a quiet so she can listen, a ribbon of pasts and futures strung together until every life is her life. What she knows she knows by not knowing, knowing the emptiness makes the bucket useful, knowing to remain a mystery to be of use. She is beyond algorithms and reverent search engine results. She will forever be only what we need to know and nothing more, like the clearest water in the deepest lake, you need only to dip your hand so far to take a drink.

"That's quite the observation…on her part and yours."

"Yeah, that's the thing with Lucy, she never really tells you anything, she just sort of, I don't know, I guess it's the same with you Hannelore, you sort of clear the way through all our bullshit so we can see things."

"I think to love someone is to know them, and what could be more important than to know ourselves."

"I don't know if I'll ever get there."

"No?"

"When I look at myself, all I see is all the fucked up shit."

"Michael…"

"Sorry…I don't know how else to say it…"

"You had a profound experience, an experience that will likely change you forever, but that doesn't mean that your past is gone."

"What difference does it make if I can see myself, if…I don't know, like how do I not keep being the old me…do people really change?"

"Yes…yes they do. You've already changed…"

"I don't know, I…"

"Michael, don't expect that the work is done, it's never

done, for any of us. The truth is, just like that scar under your chin, your past is there with you, that's not going to change, but you can change. You have changed."

"I hope so..."

"You don't sound so convinced."

"I'm just scared I'll keep doing the same shit."

"It's okay to be afraid."

"Is it?"

"You told me once that fear's a good motivator."

"Yeah, I learned that much bouncing in Cleveland."

"Well, now you can use the vigilance you developed to work for you instead of against you."

"I don't know what I'd do without you, Hannelore."

"It's a long life, Michael, and your's is an especially long path, but don't shortchange yourself, you've had to come a long way to be here, longer than most, but that's to your advantage."

"Yeah, I didn't have much of a head start, I guess."

"It's a gift, really. It's built a degree of empathy in you that's really quite extraordinary...your friend and those firemen are alive today because of it."

"It's better to be lucky, than good."

"Luck is what we make of it, Michael, your whole life readied you for that moment, No regrets, okay?"

"I don't know, that's a pretty big ask."

"The entirety of our lives, the good and the bad, make us who we are, and who you are is what carried those seven lives down the mountain."

AFTER ENLIGHTENMENT
FLOOR STILL NEED SWEPT

PEKING NOODLE CO

I don't believe in love at first sight. I loved Kelli the moment I saw her. I sometimes think I'd known her forever, like she was already a ghost when we met, and what was I, but a big empty house to haunt. I don't know what she thought back then or at the end. I don't know what love is really, but I seem to know when I'm in it or without. Everything that burns burns out, that much I do know, even the best of luck will only carry you so far. But that's the thing about luck, we always want to think it's something else, some bit of fate or God's grace, destiny in some grand design, divine, like luck's not enough. And still it's the desperate that look up and ask God to show them the way, and the lucky looking around, not watching where they're going and getting there just the same. It is the way of heaven when there is no other way, and the way of luck after that.

I'm here now where she went, where we stopped, where she started over again. This is where I sit now, where she sat, a cheap IKEA kitchen chair or a stiff couch that looks better than it is to sit on. This is where I stand now, where she stood to put on her face, a dull bathroom mirror above a weary wall sink, a single bulb ceiling fixture above everything else. I always told her she didn't need it, the makeup, and secretly loved that her fresh washed face was mine and no one else's. Now it's my pared down face in the medicine cabinet mirror, waiting for the hot water to run hot, testing it with my finger, watching the water die down the drain, wondering if it will ever rain again or if it's too late if it does.

This is where I lie down now, where she laid down, the lonely double mattress she left behind, too big for just me and too small for two. I breathe into the air where she breathed, in and finally out, in the dust of the day and in her pretty sleep. This is where I dream, where she dreamed, and wake up each morning with the havoc of feral parrots outside on the line and polite Westside street traffic, a post war apartment on Fifth and California, a bright corner building of stucco and wood, everything faded by the years of sun and salt air, everything painted over the same color so it seems like nothing ever happened.

The little man is here, he has worked here for years, so many years no one can even see him, only seeing what he's done when he's done, only noticing him once he's gone and the noise has stopped. He comes each week to cut the grass between the building and the sidewalk and the sidewalk and the street, to water the courtyard palms and plants and see that the bougainvillea bracts and tree leaves are blown into a pile with the grimy blower he's brought and picked up and put in the green bin in the alley like a church's dirty secret. Saint Monica's ringing two blocks up the street.

"Hey man, how's it going?"

The little man won't speak, but nod, his small eyes on mine only long enough to look away, long enough for me to see him and to his end. It runs through me like a childhood fear, a hot electric stab of a memory not mine, but remembered still, something so cold it feels hot. It stops my next breath and my next step, everything stops but the grind of metal against concrete in my head, a lack of air in my lungs, an emptiness beneath my heart to my backbone, his death blurted out in front of me, painted red and the blackest blue and oil cast. He will die today on the freeway, he will take the freeway instead of the canyon road to the Valley, the canyon road closed from the fire he lit. His small blue Ford Ranger will be pushed over the line by a clumsy box truck driven by a delivery driver absently eating a Subway sandwich until the little man's Ford hits head on into the concrete divider where the PCH turns and turns into the 10 in the McClure Tunnel heading east, the way west, the way to the pure land, pushing back the other way.

"Are you okay, dear?"
"Uhhh, yeah…yeah…I'm good."
"You poor thing, you look like you just saw a ghost."
"It's been a long week."
"I know I haven't felt myself with all these awful fires. Thank God the winds have finally stopped, but the smoke is still just terrible. The radio news said the air is worse than anytime in Los Angeles, even worse than the seventies."

"Yeah, it's pretty bad."

"I remember walking the boys to school back then, you could hardly see the mountains through the smog, we were close enough to walk, that's why Barry and I wanted the house on Irving so bad, we were close to the school and his work at the MGM studios."

"The air is pretty bad, I should let you get inside."

"...Barry did all the lighting for the movies, thirty-seven years he worked there, they all loved Barry, all the famous directors and the movie stars...they'd all ask for him because they knew no one would make them look better, that's what they'd say...'get me Barry Kane,' God rest his soul, my Barry..."

"Are you okay with that cart?"

"Oh yes, I roll it right up to the bottom step and I take the bags out one by one from there. I probably should just go to the Von's, the farmers market is getting so expensive, but I like walking around and seeing everything, it's like being in Paris. I've never been oversees, but I like to imagine that's what Paris looks like, all the fruits and vegetables laid out in their little stands and the bread and the cheese people and the fish man. It's a whole wonderful world all in one place."

"Yeah, Santa Monica is pretty hard to beat...why don't you let me help you with your bags, I'm Michael, we met a few weeks ago, I'm right across from you in number 8."

"Good lord, here I am going on and on and I didn't even recognize you, I need new glasses, but still, such silliness.... How are you and Katie?"

"Kelli."

"Yes, of course, Kelli, have the two of you moved back in?"

"It's just me."

"Oh, I hope the two of you aren't having problems. Being just married can be challenging. I remember when Barry and I first married, I loved him to death, but it was hard living with another person with all their particular habits and comings and goings and such. I was just nineteen years old and I'd never lived with a man, I mean other than my father, I was one of four girls and our mother, living with a man was a very new experience. Our first night Barry turned on the fan in the bedroom, it was March and you know how cold it can be in March. Turns out Barry could only sleep if there was a fan on, middle of winter and he has the fan on, but God rest his soul, he was a good man and I loved him and I learned to live with things. The two of you will be just fine."

"Kelli won't be coming back."

"Give her time, dear, I'm sure you'll work things out. Barry and I have been married for…I'm just so bad with numbers, our wedding was March second the year Mr. Shepherd went into space, that was 1961…so we've been married for…oh, math was never my strong suit…"

"'When did Barry pass away?"

"Barry left us in 2002, God rest his soul."

"So forty-two years."

"Well, we're still married, dear. My Barry might not be here, but he has eternal life in heaven, I'm sure of that, he was a dear, kind, good man…and very handsome, people thought he looked just like Keir Dullea…"

"Ok, then…uh Sixty-two years and counting."

"That's most of my life, I married so young. I miss him dearly, of course, but I'm happy, I'm living here the best I can on my own until I'm with him again. I miss the house, but it was too much for just me. I know Barry's watching over me and the boys…I can't imagine if we weren't still married when I see him in heaven, it would be horribly awkward."

"Barry's a lucky, man."

"He always treated me like a queen. Oh listen to me going on and on…"

"It's fine, it's a great love story, the two of you…come on now, let me help you with your groceries."

"That's very sweet of you, dear. And don't you worry yourself, every couple have their little tiffs. I'm sure Kelly can see what a good heart you have, that's why you love her…. We fall in love with the people who see us."

"Yeah, I guess we do…wow, that's a lot of pomegranates."

"I'm so silly, I'll never eat all of them, but they were all so beautiful…I just couldn't stop myself…take some…for you and Kelly. Some people say that a pomegranate was the forbidden fruit in the Garden of Eden, not an apple. I don't doubt it, pomegranates just seem like something from heaven, don't you think?"

"Yeah, they really are beautiful."

"Apples, well God forgive me if I sound judgmental, but apples…look to me to be something that would grow in your backyard…"

A DAY CAN CHANGE WHAT THE YEARS COULD NOT

PEKING NOODLE CO

It was the end of the continent and the end of this dreaming, this California and this salt water waiting, but the ocean seems to stop and start in the same place, everything happens at its edges. It was the end of the road, the canyon's quiet finish at the coast, an uncomplaining road sign, a two sided arrow pointing right and left, saying what you already know, saying that the way you've been going has come to an end. And yet the end of every road is the beginning of another the other way, a different dream, in a different sleep. They say we dream the entire time we're asleep, but it's only at certain times during the night that we can remember them, if we remember them.

Everything is starting again, the traffic on the Coast Highway and the waves again, at the road's edge at the beach, a brief bit of rock and sand and everything blue after that, the ocean and the sky blurring into the offing and to the end of what we can see so we're left just believing. It was the end of so many things and the beginning of something else, everything becomes something else, what Lucy says, what I say now, staring down at my blurring tattoos. It is overcast and cool like the Santa Anas never happened, but even here the weather changes just when you think it will forever be the same, just when you thought you knew her. But she knew me better than I knew myself and where would I go after all this, after her, after Los Angeles like it is, like you always thought it would be from the movies and the t.v.. This place will give you light to see and turn around and blind you, set you free and tie you tight to all the bright light hopes you have and the dreams you never want to wake from.

Kelli always dreamed of living at the beach, our canyon would be as close as she would get, all that way from a Midwest and almost, a drop of rain that would never make it to the rill. But her days were blue when it would be gray at the water. It was always bright on the mountain with what looked like a new sun each morning, what seemed secondhand before her. I could hardly tell the sun and her apart, so they were all I could see when I looked, even with a moon still in the sky from the night before, what can pull up an ocean or the will of a woman's blood, what I wouldn't notice until she was gone and the sun was on its own again.

The old stick house we thought of as ours has burnt to the ground, but for its foundation and the found rock chimney stone and mortar, the steel of appliances and other non-combustible odds and ends. The Sheriff's Department has the canyon closed except for residents, what's open nine to three with a Topanga address on a picture ID, to see what's gone and to sift through what's left, what's left something different than before. Everything is different than before. I go up everyday and kick around what was her and me, and to water the trees, only the oaks are left, all their leaves are gone, their trunks and limbs pitch from the fire. But the folks that know say they're alive still and will grow green again despite the scars. Trees native to these mountains are privy to the promise of fire.

Everything else is mostly gone, the consequence of a kind of luck. Everything that was us is ash or atom and on a different path now. There's something beautiful about it, the mountain clean of our human clutter, black and barren, but for the leafless trees and the aspirations of their roots, verdant dreams in the new ground rich with the remains of all that took from it before. I've lost everything, but I'm not sure what I really had, this life's not for keeping. It seems what lasts is what you give away and let go. And still I find a comfort in the ashes, even if it's something else, it is something, and a sort of keepsake of all that was before. I bought a flat shovel to shovel and a stone rake to rake through the muddle and the mislay, what our life together came to, what Hannelore says is my way of 'processing the loss,' what I say is something to do.

"Hey Lucy."
"Michael, you go to house today?"
"Yeah."
"How it go?"
"I found this..."
"Diamond..."
"It must be the stone from Kelli's engagement ring."

"It good luck, it stay with you."

"That's what's weird, I don't know where it came from. Kelli didn't leave her ring at the house…all I can figure is it was in her personal effects from the Sheriff's office. They'd put everything in a big manila envelope, besides her purse and stuff…I never opened it. Now I'm wondering if she had it on or…or if she was driving up to the house to give it back to me…"

"You can't see what you look for."

"What?"

"You can't see what you look for."

"So…I'll never see anything that I'm looking for…no matter what?"

"You look for answer about love, but love not of earth, love thing of heaven."

"So…I'll know the answer when I'm dead?"

"Lucy not know, not dead yet."

"Then what are our lives all about? I mean if we can't find the answers to anything, what the hell are we here for?"

"More question without answer."

"Jesus Lucy, you're the one always telling me I need to find my way. Well, how do I find my way if I can't ever know where I'm going?"

"You look for moon in moonless sky. If you not see something not mean it not there. Way of life not way of knowing…way of life way of believing."

"What do you mean?"

"You want to know Kellee love you, if Kellee alive…maybe tell you she love you, maybe tell you she not love you, you still not know, you not ever know, you need believe, that the way."

"I don't know...I don't know what to think."

"Not think, not know, believe...believe in you heart...not in you head."

"Well, I loved her...I still do...maybe that's what matters."

"Maybe...you not look for diamond, but find diamond. Maybe diamond find you. Either way, it good thing, good energy. Keep with you alway, the good...everything else, everything that burn away mean to go."

"Yeah, I guess so..."

"What you want eat? Shrimp in black bean sauce?"

"You know...I think I'll have the pan fried shrimp in the shell...and Kung Pao Chicken. It's weird, but I've been thinking about both of them all day. I guess that's what shoveling for six hours straight will do for you."

"Work with hand good thing, work with earth, thing of earth you can know."

"So I can know I'm hungry?"

"Yes, you belly know what you head not ever know."

"Lucy...what happened out there...in the fire?"

"Many thing burn."

"Yeah, I know that...but.... How did I see the old Lucy?"

"Not know, fire burn away thing between life and death, life easier to see close to death, maybe that explain."

"I saw something today...the landscaper at Kelli's apartment building, he's probably already dead. I watched it, the whole thing...him die...his truck hitting the wall just inside the McClure Tunnel...I'm kind of fucked up about it all, like...I don't know...like it left sort of a...like an empty space in me or something."

"Many thing happen in fire, fire change everything it touch, only make sense it change you too. You see different thing now."

"Will I see old Lucy again?"

"When Lucy old, that long time from now."

"Yeah it is."

"Did you see Lucy death?"

"I think so..."

"Good, now we even...go sit regular table, look at fish, good to look at fish, lower blood pressure."

"Ok, Lucy, whatever you say..."

The long fish swims in a circle, what seems like a line, like it's going somewhere, but it knows better, going nowhere, if you know where you're going, you're already there. Luck is like that and Los Angeles, so you always think you're getting somewhere even with the traffic. Even with my eyes closed I can feel the sun on my face, like her first kiss again, what I think I remember and how I've forgotten the last. She was like that, mountains at the edge of everything and an ocean and a different shade of blue, a canyon that starts and stops at the water, a space between the mountains that is the beginning and the ending of all my dreaming, a long valley after that with its own sort of sun, and mountains again on the other side. All of it a kind of beautiful so you always only see the best of her no matter where you look, and you will look because you have to, and you will love her because there is no other way.

And if love is not of knowing, but believing, then love is what I say. If you ever loved me, then you love me still...

**HEARTS DON'T CHANGE
MINDS DO**

PEKING NOODLE CO

About the Author

Brian David Cinadr, born and raised in Cleveland, Ohio, and based now with his family in the coastal mountains of southern and central California. His life is storied with strippers and studio executives, mafia businessmen and neighborhood pushers. He has had a career in bodybuilding, dug graves, paved roads, and worked as a bodyguard for rock stars and Hollywood celebrities. Cinadr's debut novel, *there seemed a river*, was a 2020 Amazon #1 new release, an IAN Book of the Year Finalist, the 2022 Global Book Award Silver Medal winner in world fiction, and the 2021 eLit Bronze Medal winner for Best Literary Fiction. His short stories have been published in a variety of journals, ranging from The *Alaska Quarterly* to *ZYZZYVA*. He is the recipient of Cal State Northridge's Best Short Fiction, 2003, and is a two-time Pushcart Award nominee for America's Best Short Fiction. Cinadr's stories grow out of his rust belt roots, gleaned from the factories and fields of his childhood, from the highways that gave him hope and a vague faith in God and an America that haunt him still.